READ.
IF YOU
DARE

READ.

IF YOU
DARE

TWELVE TWISTED TALES
FROM THE EDITORS
OF READ MAGAZINE

The Millbrook Press
Brookfield, Connecticut

Published by The Millbrook Press, Inc.
2 Old New Milford Road
Brookfield, Connecticut 06804

Copyright © 1997 by Weekly Reader Corporation
Printed in the United States of America
All rights reserved
Lib. ed. 6 5 4 3 2 1
Pbk. ed. 6 5 4 3 2 1
Library of Congress Cataloging-in-Publication Data
Read if you dare : twelve twisted tales from the editors of Read Magazine.
p.   cm.
Summary: A collection of stories by such authors as Nathaniel Hawthorne,
Ambrose Bierce, and Stephen King, exploring the notions of fate, destiny, and
coincidence.
ISBN 0-7613-0046-5 (lib. bdg.). — ISBN 0-7613-0343-X (pbk.)
1. Fate and fatalism—Juvenile fiction. 2. Children's stories, American.
[1. Fate and fatalism—Fiction. 2. Short stories.] I. Read magazine.
PZ5.T88   1997
[Fic]—dc20 96-44221 CIP   AC

Book design by Tania Garcia

ACKNOWLEDGMENTS

"Battleground" by Stephen King. Reprinted with permission. © Stephen King. All rights reserved.

"Deadline" by Richard Matheson. Reprinted by permission of Don Congdon Associates, Inc. © 1960 by Richard Matheson.

"Night Burial" by Ken Siebert. Reprinted by permission of the author.

"Reverse Insomnia" by Jonathon Blake. Reprinted by permission of the author.

"The Right Kind of House" by Henry Slesar. Reprinted by permission of the author.

"The Ruum" by Arthur Borges. Reprinted by permission of the author and the author's agents, Scott Meredith Literary Agency, L.P., 845 Third Avenue, New York, NY 10022.

"Skater" by Catherine Gourley was inspired by the poem "The Skater of Ghost Lake" by William Rose Benét.

"Snow Cancellations" by Donald R. Burleson. Reprinted by permission of the author.

Read is a literature magazine published for students in middle and senior high school by the Weekly Reader Corporation. Published biweekly during the school year, the magazine features the best of contemporary young adult fiction and nonfiction with classical literature adaptations and historical theme issues. The Best of *Read* series celebrates the magazine's fiftieth anniversary.

INTRODUCTION

The ancient Greeks believed that Night and Air united and gave birth to the three Fates. Robed in white, the three sisters determine the destiny of all humans. Clotho is the spinner of life. For each man and woman, she spins a fine linen thread on her spindle. Lachesis is the measurer of life. She determines the worth of the linen thread, deciding if it will be woven into goodness or evil. Atropos, the shearer of life, is the smallest and most terrible of the sisters. She determines how long each mortal's life will be, then with her sharp shears snips the linen thread.

Some mortals greatly feared the Fates. Others scoffed at the sway the Fates supposedly held over mortals. Still others believed that the Fates could be tempted and the linen threads of life twisted, if only just a little.

In celebration of fifty years of publishing, the editors of *Read* are proud to bring you this collection of tales, each a twist of fate. We have blended contemporary young adult short stories with literary classics. What the stories—both classic and contemporary—have in common is this: Each has appeared in the pages of *Read* over the years and each tells a tale of a person who faces an unexpected turn of events. But is the unexpected simply a coincidence or is it destiny? Are the mortals in these tales innocent victims of circumstance? Or have they tempted the Fates and brought the dreaded twist upon themselves?

Read on … if you dare.

CONTENTS

PART I — CLOTHO, SPINNER OF LIVES

SKATER   19
by Catherine Gourley

NIGHT BURIAL   35
by Ken Siebert

SNOW CANCELLATIONS   49
by Donald R. Burleson

THE RUUM   63
by Arthur Porges

CONTENTS

PART II — LACHESIS, WEAVER OF GOOD AND EVIL

A MEETING WITH DEATH   79
by Geoffrey Chaucer

THE BIRTHMARK   91
by Nathaniel Hawthorne

ARRESTED   101
by Ambrose Bierce

THE RIGHT KIND OF HOUSE   105
by Henry Slesar

BATTLEGROUND   117
by Stephen King

CONTENTS

PART III — ATROPOS, TRIMMER OF THREADS

THE BARGAIN   137
A retelling of the Greek myth
of Admetus and the Shadow of Death

REVERSE INSOMNIA   141
by Jonathon Blake

DEADLINE   149
by Richard Matheson

PART I
CLOTHO,
SPINNER OF LIVES

SKATER

by Catherine Gourley

She said his name as if she had known him forever,
as if they were already good friends.

The air is December-cold on Ghost Lake, but Jeremy Randall's cheeks are hot and flushed. He grunts as he elbows the other skaters away from the puck. Their shouts echo across the frozen lake. The puck spins free of the tangle of hockey sticks and bladed feet, skidding out beyond the dock. The boys chase the rubber disk, a blur now in the growing darkness of late afternoon. The score is tied, and the game is in sudden-death overtime. Whoever makes the next goal wins.

Jeremy reaches the puck first. Shaving ice, he pivots, then skates the puck back toward shore. In an instant, he slaps the puck. It whizzes past the goalie's legs.

"Yes!" Jeremy shouts. He holds his arms high in victory as Don and Hugh leave the ice. His jacket, like theirs, is tossed on the lakeshore, but Jeremy skates out again beyond the dock. His movements are effortless, the blades like wings on his feet.

A sudden wind bends the tops of the fir trees fringing the far shore. Like the echo of a crying bird, the wind whips across the frozen lake, but Jeremy doesn't hear its moan or feel its sting. Orange and violet streaks darken the sky minute by minute, but Jeremy doesn't notice that either. Instead, he hears again the whack of his hockey stick and sees the puck skid into the goal. At that moment, Jeremy is his own hero, and he shouts into the wind, "I could skate forever!" He imagines himself in Chicago in a brightly lit arena, wearing a Blackhawk uniform and circling the ice to earsplitting cheers from thousands of fans. "Jer! Jer! Jer!" Chicago Stadium vibrates with the noise.

"Jer!" Don cups his hands around his mouth and calls again, "Jer!"

Jeremy looks over his shoulder. On shore, Don and Hugh seem far, far away. Jeremy digs in and starts back.

That's when he sees her.

She is kneeling in the snow in a small clearing, not far from the public beach where Don and Hugh are waiting. She rises and steps onto the ice. She is dressed in white; otherwise, Jeremy might not have seen her in the almost darkness.

Jeremy turns and skates backward so he can watch

her. He skates slowly now, but she is too far away for him to see her face.

"Jer! C'mon. We're going!"

Jeremy turns again and skates to shore. "Did you see that girl?" He sits on the frozen ground and quickly unlaces a skate.

"What girl?"

Jeremy looks across the lake, but the white figure is gone, hidden perhaps behind the trees on the point. Only the dark shadow of a bird sweeps across the ice now. "There was a girl," Jeremy says, pulling off the other skate. "Out there. Just coming onto the ice."

"No one comes to Ghost Lake after dark," says Hugh.

"Especially not a girl," says Tom. "Alone."

The two boys start along the path through the trees to the park road. The last threads of orange and violet light melt into the ebony ice and trees. From where he stands, Jeremy cannot see even the end of the dock now.

"But I saw her." He speaks out loud. "Didn't I?"

Later, at home in his room, Jeremy lies on his bed and stares at the poster of Mario Lemieux on the wall. He studies the grim determination in the hockey player's face. He can almost feel the adrenaline pumping through Mario's veins as he battles for control of the puck.

"Jer?"

Jeremy's mother opens the door, breaking the dream.

She has just come home from work. "How was school today?" she asks.

Jeremy shrugs. "School's school."

She steps inside the room, decorated with professional hockey memorabilia. At first, she was happy about her son's interest in the sport. It got his mind off the divorce, and a year ago, when she and Jeremy moved back to Pennsylvania from Chicago, hockey was an easy way for Jeremy to make new friends. Now she worries that hockey is the only thing her son thinks about.

"Did you spend some time with your grandfather this afternoon?" she asks.

"Poppy was asleep when I got home." Then, unable to avoid his mother's penetrating stare, Jeremy admits, "I kind of got home late."

She crosses her arms in front of her. "Playing hockey, right?"

Jeremy grins. "I really smoked them. I made a slapshot the length of the whole dock!"

"Weren't you going to do something for me and Poppy today?"

Jeremy looks at her with innocent eyes. "What?"

"You know Poppy can't climb a ladder anymore."

"Oh yeah. The Christmas lights."

His mother turns for the door. "Do it now, Jer."

Years ago, his mother had told him about the winter solstice and how burning candles in the windows was an ancient custom urging the sun to burn brightly on the shortest day of the year—December 21. Jeremy gets up, but he sighs deeply to let his mother know that he's too old now for trees and tinsel, colored lights and superstitions.

☠

Jeremy pokes through the boxes in Poppy's attic, looking for the decorations. He has lived with his grandfather only since January, and so things in the house are still new for him. He finds the box of Christmas lights and digs deeper to find the extra bulbs. As his hand pushes through a tangle of wires, he sees an old card and picks it out of the box.

It is a Christmas postcard, yellow with age. Bits of silver glitter stick to the snow scene. Suddenly, Jeremy recognizes the place as Ghost Lake. In the picture, fir trees line the shore. Even the old dock is there. Printed in red-ribboned letters across the winter sky are the words *Season's Greetings!*

He is about to toss the card back into the box when he notices the girl. In the picture, she is kneeling in the snow in the clearing, lacing up her skates. He flips the card over. It is addressed to George Mellon, Jeremy's grandfather. The written message—*I can't wait to see you again. Love, Cecily*—makes Jeremy slightly uncomfortable, as if he is peeking through a keyhole at Poppy's life. The date

☠

on the card is December 14, 1922. Something inside Jeremy Randall quickens, like wings batting against his chest. Today is December 14 — seventy-five years later!

He stares at the picture again. The girl is wearing a long coat trimmed in white fur. "It's her!" Jeremy says out loud.

"Who?" His mother is coming up the attic steps with two mugs of hot chocolate.

Quickly, though he is not sure why, Jeremy slips the postcard into his hip pocket. He turns and lifts the rope of Christmas lights to show his mother. "I got them, spare bulbs and all."

"Good," she says. She settles down in the nest of boxes on the floor. She spies an angel tree topper with yellow fiberglass hair. "Oh, look at this!" she cries happily. "These ornaments have been in my family for years," she says, talking more to herself now than to Jeremy.

After a few minutes, he quietly leaves his mother alone with her memories.

☠

Late the next day, Jeremy stands in the shadows of the steep firs at Ghost Lake. He is not surprised when the girl appears again in the clearing. As before, she kneels to lace up her skates. He watches as the wind ripples the white fur collar on her coat. She steps onto the ice, glides in a wide circle, and then, step-over-step, gains speed. She twists, leaping gracefully into the air, and lands on one skate, gliding backward.

On the next jump, she lands off-balance and falls, hard. Jeremy rushes out of the shadows and, flat-soled, runs across the ice to help her. "Are you all right?" he asks.

Her cheeks are flushed—from the cold or from the exercise, Jeremy isn't sure which. Thin streams of late afternoon sun fall through the trees and glitter like tinsel in her dark hair. She's beautiful, Jeremy thinks, amazed.

"Were you spying on me?" she asks angrily.

"No! No, I was just...." He turns and points at the trees. "I was just walking and...." He faces her again. "Yeah, I guess I was spying on you."

"You're Jeremy," she says. When he looks surprised, she laughs. "I've been spying on you, too. You play hockey after school. You're good."

Jeremy grins, embarrassed but pleased, too. "You're Cecily," he says, remembering Poppy's Christmas postcard.

If she is surprised that he also knows her name, she doesn't show it. "I'm visiting my grandfather. His name is John Culver. He's an artist. Do you know him?"

Jeremy shakes his head. "I'm kind of new around here."

A sudden rush of wings startles them, but it is only an owl circling low over the ice. "You shouldn't skate here alone at night," Jeremy says protectively.

"Oh, I'm not alone," she laughs, her voice like a bird's.

"Why do you think they call it Ghost Lake, Jer?"

She says his name like she has known him forever, like they are already good friends. "Wait here," he tells her. "My skates are on shore. I'll go with you."

The next morning at breakfast, Jeremy asks his mother if she knows John Culver. She looks up from the newspaper. "John Culver? Who told you about John Culver?"

"He's some kind of painter, right?"

"He was. John Culver has been dead for years."

Again, Jeremy feels the wings of a nervous bird fluttering inside his ribs. "He's dead? But he can't be!"

"But he is. He was an old man when I was a kid growing up here. We used to call him 'the hermit.' He lived over by the lake. Poppy warned me not to go there, but I always did." Jeremy's mother looks curiously at her son. "Why?"

Jeremy pulls the postcard from his pocket. "I found this in the attic."

"Pretty," she says. "And look! It was painted by him, see?" She points a fingernail at John Culver's name printed in the corner. She turns the card over. "Whoever sent this to Poppy sent it seventy years ago when Poppy was—"

"Fifteen," Jeremy says. "My age." He'd figured that out the night he found the card. "Grandma's name wasn't Cecily, was it?"

"No," says Jeremy's mother, amused at having discovered a secret love of Poppy's. "It definitely wasn't!"

"Then... who *was* Cecily?"

"I've no idea, but your grandfather was a handsome man once," she says. "Just like you. And he loved to skate, just like you do."

His mother crosses to the refrigerator and uses a decorative magnet to tack the card on the door. "It's our first card of the season. Kind of like getting a holiday hello from the past, isn't it?" She smiles at the picture. "I like it."

Jeremy says nothing. His mother would never believe him if he told her that he had been skating with that same girl from the postcard last night on Ghost Lake.

☠

"Why didn't you tell me your grandfather was dead?" Jeremy asks Cecily late that afternoon at the lake.

Her voice is sad. "Because I don't think of him as being dead. I prefer to remember him the way he was when he was alive. What's wrong with that?"

Jeremy regrets now bringing it up. It doesn't matter about John Culver. He takes her hand and they skate together.

The moon, already risen, is pale in the sky. But as night deepens, the moon glows into life like a candle in a window celebrating the solstice. It casts the bird-like shadows of Jeremy Randall and Cecily Culver on the ice. Cold crackles in the trees. Jeremy feels Cecily's fingers tighten

☠

around his hand. "You aren't scared, are you?" he asks.

"No," she answers. "Just a little cold."

☠

"Who put this here?" Surprised, Poppy turns and looks at Jeremy.

"Mom thought you'd like to see it. I found it in the attic."

Jeremy stares at his grandfather, a thin man now with white hair. His eyes are a watercolor blue, like Jeremy's own. Jeremy remembers what his mother said about Poppy being handsome and strong once and loving to skate. As Poppy stares at the picture on the postcard, his annoyance melts away.

"Who is she, Poppy?"

"An old friend," he answers quietly.

"Did you love her?"

Poppy smiles sadly. "I thought I did. But her father wouldn't let anybody near her. No one was good enough for Cecily Culver."

Then Poppy looks up, willing the memory away. He is about to toss the card into the garbage, but Jeremy stops him. "Don't!" Poppy looks at him, surprised. "She's back," Jeremy says. "I mean, her granddaughter is back. She's staying at the lake."

Poppy's eyes go wide. "What?"

☠

"Her name is Cecily, too."

"No, Cecily Culver couldn't have had a granddaughter."

"Why not?"

"Because...." Poppy hesitates. Jeremy stares at him, waiting. "Because I was with her on the ice when it happened."

"When what happened, Poppy?" Jeremy says, exasperated.

"The ice cracked. I tried to save her, but she slipped out of my hands. I ran for help, but it was too late."

An eerie feeling shivers through Jeremy. "You mean, she died?"

"Her father blamed me. He never forgave me." Poppy looks at the card in his hands, then at Jeremy. In one quick movement, he rips the card in half.

"What are you doing?" Jeremy cries.

Poppy tosses the two pieces of the card into the garbage. "Don't go there again, Jer," warns Poppy. "Stay away from that place." His grandfather walks from the room.

At first, Jeremy is too stunned to move. But a few minutes later, he goes to the wastebasket and retrieves the two pieces of the card. Alone in his room, he tapes the pieces together again.

Jeremy doesn't listen to Poppy. He goes back to Ghost Lake at dusk and waits for Cecily. For four days, they meet secretly on the shore. Arms laced together, they skate, and skate, and skate. Sometimes she sings.

Sometimes she tells him stories. "Do you know about Alcyone and King Ceyx?"

"No," he says, not embarrassed.

"They lived in ancient Greece and they were in love," Cecily says. "Like us."

Jeremy stops skating and stares at her with nervous surprise. "What did you say?"

Cecily giggles and skates away. He chases her and catches her around the waist. "What did you say?" he teases. "Tell me what you said."

"He drowned," she says at last, seriously.

"Who?"

"King Ceyx. And Alcyone was so sad that she threw herself into the sea and drowned, too."

Abruptly, Jeremy turns away from her. "I don't like that story."

Now it is Cecily who follows him across the ice. "But it's not over. Zeus felt so sorry for them that on the night of the winter solstice, he turned them into birds—kingfishers—and they lived forever."

"It's late. I gotta go." Jeremy turns for shore.

Still, Cecily follows him. "But the story has a happy ending, Jer."

He turns then and says sharply, "Don't talk about drowning, OK? You don't know what happened out here a long time ago. Poppy told me—"

"Poppy? Your grandfather?"

Jeremy stares at her, so pretty, so perfect like a picture. Still, he is not sure who Cecily really is and why she would lie to him about being John Culver's granddaughter.

She steps forward to touch his cold, unmittened hand. "Don't be mad at me," she says.

"I'm not mad. I'm just..." Suddenly, he feels a little frightened of her. He moves away from her touch.

"I'm leaving," she says then.

"What?"

"We're going home. Tomorrow will be our last night together, Jer."

They step off the ice and begin to remove their skates. Jeremy's hands are numb. He fumbles with the laces. He hadn't thought that one day Cecily might not be here. His head spins. He wants to tell her he is sorry for shouting at her. He wants to ask her if she really meant it when she said she loved him. But no words come out.

"Meet me here tomorrow," Cecily says, standing. Her skates are tied over her shoulder.

"Cecily, wait!" Jeremy is still fumbling with his own shoes, but she disappears into the shadows of the firs.

☠

It is late afternoon. The hockey game is not even close. Jeremy misses an easy shot, and Hugh shouts at him.

☠

When the game is over, they leave him behind, shaking their heads. "What's gotten into him lately?" Tom asks. Hugh shrugs.

It is the night of the winter solstice, and darkness comes early to Ghost Lake. The dim moon rises above the trees. Alone now, Jeremy skates out beyond the dock. His eyes search for the gleam of moonlight on her winged feet. He listens hard for the skurring sound of her skates, but hears only a crisp, thin sound—like a violin. It drifts on a bluish mist from the lake's far shore.

"Only a bird," he says out loud.

He leans forward into the wind as he skates, one long stride after another. "What if she doesn't come?" he thinks. No girl has ever told Jeremy Randall that she loved him, and he doesn't want to lose her the way Poppy lost his Cecily years ago.

Then he sees her. She moves from tree to tree, then kneels in the snow and laces her skates.

They join arms, and they skate. All day in front of his bedroom mirror, he has practiced what he wants to tell her. But now that she is laced to his side, he can't remember a word. He says without looking at her, "I don't want you to go."

"You don't?" Her breath is a frosty feather close to his cheek.

"Can't you stay a little longer?"

"Maybe you could come with me," she says.

He shakes his head. "How can I?"

Suddenly, over her shoulder, he sees a large shadow. It flits and swoops, startling him.

"What is it?" she asks, not letting him go.

"Nothing." Then he teases her. "Maybe a ghost. Why do you think they call it Ghost Lake?"

But Cecily doesn't laugh.

The shadow swoops again, nudging them farther away from shore.

"Jeremy?"

"It's just a bird," he says. "An owl probably."

"Or," she whispers, "a kingfisher."

He changes direction, pointing north of the dock. But the shadow follows, gliding between them and the shore.

Then he hears it. The skurring of steel following closely behind him. He skates faster, bringing Cecily with him. But the skurring comes faster, too.

"Jeremy!" Her voice is frightened now that they are far, far from the dock. Into the blue mist Jeremy skates to escape the phantom.

Then, suddenly, the ice seems to light up beneath them in jagged bolts, shooting forward and sideways. The ice crackles and pops. A split second later, a roar fills their ears.

Then all is quiet again. Only the shadows of two night birds sweep low over the frozen lake to the far shore.

☠

"Jer?"

His mother knocks on his bedroom door. It is after nine o'clock, and it is not like Jeremy to be so late getting home. She pushes the door open, feels for the light switch on the wall, and flips it on.

The room is as it was this morning when she left for work. She picks up a sweatshirt tossed on the bed and folds it. As she opens the bureau drawer to put it away, she spies Poppy's postcard. It has been ripped and taped together again. The girl is still there and the boy too, skating on Ghost Lake.

Something is different about the picture, but Jeremy's mother can't quite place it. She shrugs and turns away, leaving the light on for Jeremy when he comes home.

☠

NIGHT BURIAL

by Ken Siebert

*Terry wanted to explore the unknown. Sure,
it was risky, but someone with guts and
brains—and planning—could pull it off.*

Terry heaved the last shovelful of dirt aside, then
jumped into the three-foot hole he and Sara had just
dug. "Do you think it should be deeper?" he asked, looking up at her.

"It's deep enough," she said and dropped her shovel. In
the moonlight that filtered through the pine trees, he
thought he saw her shiver.

"You're right," he said. "Deep enough." He scrambled
out of the hole again. "Ready for the box now?" he asked.

"I don't know about this," Sara said suddenly. "Now
that we've dug the hole and I can actually see how long
and deep it is...."

"I know," he said grinning. "It makes it real."

"Terry, I'm scared."

"So am I, a little. But that's the whole point. If there's no risk, why do it?"

"Why *are* you doing this?"

"Why does somebody go over Niagara Falls in a barrel? Why did Harry Houdini let himself be handcuffed, nailed inside a crate, and lowered into a river?"

"What you're doing is different."

He grinned. "I know."

"Let's just forget it and go home. OK, Terry?"

"No way. I started this, and I'm going to finish it. Just think of it as, well, an experiment."

A chill wind swirled through the branches of the pines. Sara hugged herself. "And what if the experiment fails?"

"Look. I've explained it all to you before. Houdini didn't jump into a tank of water with his arms and legs locked in chains and then just hope he could get them unlocked in time. He practiced. He built up his endurance. He thought of every possibility ahead of time. That's why he was so brilliant."

"And you're sure you thought of everything?"

"Of course I have. I wouldn't be doing this if I wasn't ready. I'm not stupid." He looked at his watch. The red numbers glowed 9:25. "Let's get the box. I want everything in place by ten o'clock, just the way we planned."

Reluctantly, Sara followed him across the graveyard to

where she had parked her father's truck outside the gate. Belden Park was a small, old burial ground. A high wrought-iron fence enclosed the two dozen graves. Time and weather had bleached the faces of the stone markers. The names of the dead could be read on only a few stones. No one used the cemetery for burials anymore. That was why Terry had chosen this place. It was part of his plan. No one ever came to Belden Park, so no one would interfere with his experiment.

The idea had come to him during the summer, when he'd read a biography of Harry Houdini. Houdini, considered the world's greatest magician, had been more than just a trickster who created illusions. He had been a powerful athlete who had conditioned his body to do amazing things—he could dislocate his shoulders in order to slip out of a straitjacket. Houdini had made himself a master artist. There wasn't any magic about his stunts. Terry wanted to be like him.

The challenge was to test his resolve. His feat would be the ultimate contest between willpower and emotion. That was the most important point. Even someone as great as Houdini, who had a hundred different stunts, must have been scared when he had himself tied into a straitjacket and lowered headfirst from the eaves of a New York City skyscraper. To escape, he had to defeat his emotions. If he panicked, he was a dead man.

It was simple, really—if he could remain calm and under control while buried alive for eight hours, he could handle anything. Strong people didn't take the easy road. They were always testing themselves, building their inner power. Eight hours wasn't all that long if you were mentally tough.

In a sense, the experience would be a controlled nightmare. He would tape-record his reactions. When it was all over, he would play the tapes in the comfort of his bedroom and coolly analyze the experience.

For weeks, he had planned every detail, right down to the heavy rubber tubing that would be his lifeline. He needed Sara's help, of course. Even Houdini had had an assistant. No one was more reliable than Sara. She would dig him up on schedule—8:00 A.M. sharp.

Even if there was some unforeseen delay, there would be enough water if he rationed it. And there would always be plenty of air coming through the tube.

☠

At the cemetery gate, Terry checked everything a final time—blankets, a full canteen, the rubber tubing, a pillow, a cassette recorder and a tape, and a homemade, six-foot pine box. First, they carried the box and a lantern to the grave. Terry noticed with some interest that he would be lying close to Rufus James, 1850–1899, accord-

☠

ing to the tombstone. Of all the graves nearby, that one alone seemed to have been tended recently.

"Shouldn't you have some sandwiches or something?" Sara asked after they carried the rest of the gear to the newly dug grave.

"No," Terry said, "it's not exactly a picnic." He smiled at Sara, but she just looked away.

A cloud bank moved in and switched off the moon. Suddenly the night was very dark. As Sara watched Terry light a lantern, a new thought occurred to her.

"What if I stay here, right in the truck, just to make sure you're all right?"

"I'm going to be fine. I'll probably sleep most of the night away."

"Still, I'd feel a lot better if you'd let me stay and watch."

"Watch for what? This cemetery is a forgotten place. No one comes here. I've checked it out for two weeks."

"Right. All part of your perfect plan," she said.

"Sara, you don't get it. I want total isolation. It's a very important part of the experiment. Knowing you were here would wreck everything. A crowd might as well hang around and dig me up every five minutes to see how I'm doing."

Sara sighed. "Do you think the air tube is wide enough?"

"Quit worrying, will you? We tried it above ground, and it worked fine. Why should it be any different with a foot of dirt over it?"

"I can't believe we're really doing this," Sara said as Terry spread the blankets in the pine box. "We need a couple of those Houdini straitjackets."

"You think it's crazy, and I think it's an exploration."

"Of what?"

"Of me. Of who I am. I'm not like anyone else. I'm different."

That much Sara agreed with. Terry wasn't like other people. Maybe that was why she found him so attractive. Being with him was like taking a journey and not knowing what would be around the next bend.

He climbed down into the box. There was just enough room for him to stretch. "OK, now hand me the rest of the stuff."

Sara handed him the canteen of water, the pillow, the portable tape player. Then she helped him push the stiff rubber tube snugly into the hole in the lid. It was a perfect fit. No dirt could come in around it.

"That's it, I guess, Terry said. "I'll see you at eight o'clock."

Sara leaned over him. "It's not too late to change your mind," she said.

"I can't do this without you, Sara. Don't let me down. I'm counting on you."

She nodded grimly, then tried to smile. "See you in the morning."

Terry grinned. "You'd better—or I'll never speak to you again."

"That's not funny!"

Lying there, looking at the moonless sky, Terry felt a kinship with anyone who had ever explored anything first—the first person to submerge in a submarine, the first person to crawl into a space capsule. Now it was his turn to explore the unknown.

☠

Sara carefully placed the lid on top of the box and hammered a nail into each corner, leaving part of the nail-head sticking up for easy removal. Terry had said four would be enough. The air hose stuck out about a foot above ground level. As she shoveled dirt over the box, Sara was careful that no dirt got into the tube opening.

When she had finished, she knelt and spoke into the tube. "Are you OK?" She put her ear to the tube, listening. When there was no answer, she started to panic. "Terry," she yelled, "say something!"

The answer came at once. "Sweet dreams, Sara."

Sara knelt, shaking, near the fresh mound of dirt. Clouds had completely blotted the sky now, and the moon was hidden. She looked at the tombstones bathed

☠

in pale lantern light. For the first time, she began to feel a sense of violating sacred ground.

She waited a few minutes longer, listening in case Terry had changed his mind after all. But the cemetery was silent. Not even the wind was blowing now. She turned off the lantern and started toward the truck.

She sat in the cab and stared at the cemetery. The darkness had swallowed the tombstones. From where she sat, it was impossible to see that anything had been disturbed. Once more she considered spending the night in the truck. Terry would never know she was there. But it was Saturday night, and her parents expected her home by 11:00. Besides, Terry had turned down the idea, and that was that. No way could she betray his trust.

She turned on the motor and, after a final glance at the cemetery, drove toward town.

Terry lay in the black confinement, sweating from every pore. Mistake number one—not figuring on the heat. There was enough air to breathe but not enough to evaporate the perspiration. He kept brushing the sleeve of his sweater across his forehead and eyes.

He tried fanning himself. As long as he kept it up, things were a little better. When he stopped, he was right back where he started. He pressed the button on his watch, and the little red numerals sprang at him in the blackness. 12:10. Only an hour gone? Incredible.

He spoke into the recorder: "Twelve-ten, and all is not well."

He was startled by his voice, so hollow and alien. "The heat is miserable. I've got to squirm out of these clothes as much as possible. The air smells pretty bad by now. I can breathe well enough, but I'm melting. More later."

A sudden sharp cramp in his right calf made him rise up quickly and crack his forehead on the lid of the box. It hurt some, but the pain in his calf was the main concern. He tried to massage the aching muscle but couldn't reach it. After a time, the pain slowly began to ebb away.

Sweat ran in rivulets, stinging his eyes and puddling up in his ears. Mistake number two—wrong clothing. Outside, frost crystals might be forming on the blades of grass. Outside, he might have needed the sweater, the blankets.

Twisting back and forth, he tried to get out of his sweater and T-shirt. In his struggle, he used the air too quickly, and he started to black out. Giving up, he lay motionless until he slowly regained his senses. His head began to throb where he had hit it, and his drenched clothes hung to his body like leeches.

☠

Sara couldn't sleep. She had been foolish to think she could put Terry out of her mind. She could still see him, lying in that awful box, looking up at her and the moon. A dozen what-ifs ran through her mind. What if he didn't have enough air after all? What if the truck broke down as she was driving to the cemetery? What if her parents thought up some dumb chore she had to do before she left the house in the morning?

The clock on her bed table read 2:30. *Impossible!* she cried silently. She got out of bed and looked out her window. Dawn was still endless hours away.

What if he had panicked and was shouting for her?

If she took the truck now, her parents would surely hear her. She had to wait until at least 6:00. She sat on the edge of her bed, then lay back, staring at the blank ceiling of her room.

☠

Terry looked at his watch again through watery eyes. The tiny numerals danced and wavered like a red mirage— 2:45. A little more than five hours. He mustn't struggle. Getting enough air had become a serious problem.

Or was it a problem? Maybe the heat and the sweating and the suffocating lack of air were only in his imagination. Still, it seemed as if the box had somehow shrunk. Mistake number three—he hadn't realized he was claustrophobic.

He reached for the canteen and took a long drink, then cursed himself for spilling some of the precious

☠

water over his chin and neck. Still, the water gave him some relief. How stupid to misjudge the amount of heat his body would generate inside a closed box. He tried to think of Houdini, how his mind had controlled his emotions while he calmly had gone about his escape. Then something occurred to him. Houdini had died in a freak accident—someone had punched him in the stomach and burst his appendix.

What if Sara doesn't come? What if some freak accident happens to her? He pushed the button on his recorder, but the red numerals on his watch were somersaulting again. "I don't know what time it is. I must not move."

He wasn't sure why he shouldn't move. Something about air. His mind was confused. The point of the whole experiment was escaping him. Only one thought filled him.

"Sara?" he called hoarsely into the recorder. "I'm counting on you."

☠

Edith James drove to Belden Park in her old Ford with her poodle, Misty, and a large potted mum to put on the grave of her grandfather Rufus. She had risen before dawn, as always, and by the time she reached the old graveyard at 6:00 A.M., the first light of day was filtering through the pine trees. She loved this part of the day best of all, and she wanted to get things done early so she could get back

☠

to study her Bible lesson for the class before church.

When she was four, her father had died in World War I and had been buried somewhere in France. She'd never really known him, but she had a vague memory of him throwing her laughing into the air on her third birthday. She could not bring flowers to her father, but she could bring them to her grandfather—and in that way honor the man whose memory she would always cherish.

She drove her car to the end of the dirt road and parked near the gate. "All right, Misty," she said as she opened the door, "go have yourself a good run." Misty leaped outward and immediately began sniffing a small bush. His mistress primped for a second in the rearview mirror, patting her gray hair carefully into place. Then she took the plant and followed the dog into the cemetery.

She went straight to the grave, the one she visited every two months to keep it neat and tidy. She placed the plant with its pretty orange blossoms in front of Rufus's stone and was just beginning to say a prayer when she thought she heard a faint voice.

Turning her head, she saw the freshly dug grave. Misty was sniffing curiously, pawing a bit of the bare dirt. No one had been buried in the cemetery for years, Edith knew. She shook her head sadly. "Must be some pauper's grave," she spoke aloud. "Someone with no money buried here secretly during the night."

Again, she thought she heard a voice. She decided it must have been Misty whining in excitement or just her tired old ears playing tricks on her again. Then she saw the tube coming from the ground near the head of the grave. "What a pathetic little flower holder," she sighed. "And so empty. Well, whoever you are, you won't be forgotten today."

☠

Terry had drifted in and out of frightening dreams all through the night. His throat was raw, as if he had been yelling, but he remembered nothing about it. He fumbled for his canteen and managed to get it to his mouth. Only a few drops trickled onto his lips. Sara. There was something about Sara he should remember. He wondered whether he had been dreaming of her. His chest ached dully. Why was it so difficult to breathe? *Hang on,* he whispered to himself, but he wasn't sure why he should hang on or to what.

☠

Edith James snapped half a dozen mums from the plant she had brought for her grandfather and stuck the stems snugly into the rubber flower holder. "There," she said, standing up to admire their feathery orange heads. "That certainly brightens things up!" Satisfied, she called Misty and returned to her car.

☠

A mile or two down the road, she was quite surprised to pass a pickup truck heading the other way. A girl was driving, driving fast. A pretty young thing, but her face looked anxious as the truck flashed by. What on earth, Edith James wondered, would bring one of today's teenagers racing out here at this hour of the morning? Well, that wasn't her worry. She had plenty of time to take Misty home and then head off for Bible study.

Edith smiled gently. How nice, she thought, to have already done her good deed for the day.

SNOW CANCELLATIONS

by Donald R. Burleson

It was something all kids prayed for. But this time…

Snow wrapped around the house like the shroud of a mummy. From his bedroom window, Jamie could just make out the vague outline of the bird feeder on the edge of the deck. Beyond the backyard, the pines and spruces were snow-covered ghosts waving in the wind, nodding to each other, whispering.

It was going to be a big storm. Jamie liked that. Sort of. There was something exciting about a snowstorm burying everything. But it was also a little eerie.

Jamie heard his mother in the kitchen as she prepared breakfast. He knew better than to get in her way while she was getting herself ready for work. His father worked the early shift at the mill and had left an hour earlier. Jamie had heard him, too, outside, scraping the shovel blade on the surface of the driveway. It must have begun snowing during the night. And the air visible through the frosted window was still a frenzy of flakes, falling thick and fast.

The bedroom door opened. "Jamie? Are you awake? You should get dressed for school."

Jamie turned away from the window. "But it's snowing."

"They haven't cancelled school yet," she said and left. Jamie slipped on his jeans and went into the kitchen. The radio on the shelf over the dishwasher was turned up so his mother could hear it as she moved about the house.

"*... before it's over, folks, we expect fifteen to eighteen inches accumulation in some locations. If you have to go out, friends, give yourself a lot of extra time to get where you're going. And please drive with care. Hey, we like you and we want you to get there safe and sound. I'm Rick Phillips from Storm Center Radio, 1360 on your dial. The cancellations are coming in, and we'll have a complete rundown following these messages, so stay tuned.*"

Jamie, still half-asleep, ate his toast and watched the swirling fingers of snow tapping against the kitchen window. Maybe they were going to cancel school! He'd heard it happened up here in the north all the time. In Arizona, where his family had lived till this past year, school had never been cancelled for snow. Ever. The only time he'd ever seen snow was on that trip to Colorado when he was six.

"Maybe they'll close up at Sanborn's," Jamie called to

his mother, "and you won't have to go to work."

She shook her head ruefully as she came back into the kitchen. "Sanborn's wouldn't close if it was the end of the world."

On the radio, the commercials ended and the cancellation announcements began. Jamie set his spoon down and listened.

"*...Bedford Senior Center is open but no transportation. Hooksett, no school, all schools....*

Come on! Jamie thought, finishing his cereal. *Come on! Who cares about all that stuff? What about Merrimack?*

"*...Derry, no school. Salem, no school. Dingdong Bell Nursery School in Goffstown closed today. This just in,*"— Jamie had a feeling and held his breath— "*Merrimack, no school....*"

"Mom?"

"I heard it, Jamie."

"All right!" he cried. "No school." Suddenly, he felt very much awake. He went now to the living room window. Fresh snow had already covered the driveway where his father had shoveled. It was beautiful stuff, but somehow also darkly suggestive, as if saying: *See, you people think you're so smart, but I can shut you down anytime I feel like it, and I feel like it right now.* A snowplow turned onto his street and rumbled past, pushing a sliding hill of snow with its wide-mouth blade.

"I guess you'll have to be here by yourself," his mother said. She had her coat on and her boots.

He shrugged. "No problem."

"I guess you can watch TV or play tapes. For lunch, make yourself a peanut butter and jelly sandwich. I'll call you at lunchtime, but you know my number at work if you need me."

"OK, Mom. Bye."

Still, she hesitated. "I hate to leave you alone. Maybe I can work through my lunch hour and get home early. OK?"

"It's no big deal," he said again.

He watched as she trudged out across the drive and brushed snow off her car. She climbed in and slowly backed out. The car's taillights winked red through the wind-driven flakes and then were gone around the corner.

Now he was alone. Alone in the house, alone with the snow brushing against every window.

☠

Outside, the wind swirled and howled and slashed the snow like a torn curtain. Jamie heard the floorboards creak, and he turned. Funny, he thought, how an empty house could make sounds.

Well. He stacked his breakfast dishes in the sink, then went to his bedroom. He fumbled through the mess of

☠

socks and underwear in his dresser and uncovered his emergency supply of candy bars. Taking three, he went to his parents' bedroom.

He crawled onto the bed and arranged the sheets snugly around his legs like a bird's nest. He had decided on this room rather than his own because this room had a phone. He was going to call Kevin Riley.

He unwrapped a candy bar and took a bite and leaned across to the phone beside the bed. After tapping out Kevin's number, he straightened back out in his nest with the phone in hand. A boy's voice answered on the other end.

"'Lo?"

"Hey, Kevin, your mother sniffs gym socks."

"Cheez. Jamie, you're weird."

"Yeah, and you're a total geek."

"Hey, what are you eating?"

"Dog boogers." At this they both collapsed into laughter. Then Kevin said, "Great about school bein' closed, huh? What're you doin'?"

"Sittin' here talkin' to you on the phone. Whadda ya think I'm doin'?"

"Your folks home?"

"No," Jamie said. "Yours?"

"Naw, they both had to go to work. Wicked neat bein' home by yourself, huh?"

"Sure. Yeah, I guess so."

Kevin guffawed. "Whadda ya mean, you guess so? You scared bein' alone, Jamie?"

"No, no, I'm not scared. What's there to be scared of?" He really wasn't scared. Not exactly.

"Hey," said Kevin. "I'll tell you what's to be scared of. You're from Arizona, right? You don't know. Cars skid off the road and plough into snowbanks. People walking in a blizzard get lost all the time. They get snow-blind, and then their toes and fingers fall off from frostbite."

"Their fingers and toes fall off?" Jamie repeated incredulously.

"See you *are* scared. Go find your mommy, Jamie."

"Hey," Jamie had just realized that the radio was still going in the kitchen. "Hey, hold on. I'm gonna go get the radio and bring it in here so I can listen in bed."

"You in bed, Jamie? What a wimp."

Jamie went for the radio. When he had it plugged in and playing on his mother's bureau, he resettled himself in the middle of the bed and picked up the phone. "I want to check out the cancellations."

"How come? You already know they cancelled school. What else matters?"

Jamie watched the snow falling ever harder and faster beyond the windowpanes. "I thought if it got bad enough, they might close the mill early and—"

"And our dads would come home, right? I told you you were scared."

"Stick it in your ear, Kevin."

"What station you listenin' to?" Kevin asked. Jamie could hear him tuning a radio across the dial, a jumble of stations fading in and out.

"Got it," Kevin said, and Jamie could hear the radio sound over the phone slide into agreement with his own radio.

"*...and storm-related information continues to come in. It's a big one out there, folks, so stay with us and we'll keep you up to date as this whole region gets buried.*"

"Hey, Jamie, this is neat. The whole town's covered up with snow."

Jamie had been to Kevin's apartment building across town several times and knew that you could see just about the whole town from Kevin's fourteenth-floor living room window.

"Kevin?"

"Huh?"

"Can you see Sanborn's from there?"

"Sanborn's? Yeah, of course I can see Sanborn's. It's got snow all over the roof. What's the matter, puddin'-face, oo miss oo mommy?"

"Suck toe jam, Kevin."

"Munch navel fuzz, Jamie."

☠

They were both quiet for a while; the radios murmured the same commercials, the same chatter.

"*...cancelled, and also the meeting of the Franco-American Friendship Club for this evening has been cancelled.*"

"Hey, Kevin?"

"What?"

"Listen, you don't have to hang on the line if you got things you want to do."

A moment of silence. Then: "Naw, I don't have nothin' I want to do. I'll stay on."

Jamie said, "Sort of nice having someone to talk to, right?"

"Yeah, I guess it is, kind of. Even if I have to talk to some chickenskin like you."

They became thoughtful again, neither speaking for a good while. Outside, the snow seemed heavier, more insistent than ever. It brushed against the frosty panes with jittery fingers of white, worrying at the glass.

Then Jamie said, "We never had this stuff in Arizona. Something about it is kind of eerie, huh?" Jamie steeled himself for Kevin's smart-mouth reply.

But Kevin was slow in replying, and surprisingly he said, "Yeah, kind of."

What do you know, Jamie thought, *he feels it too.* "Kevin, can you see the mill?"

☠

"Yeah, just barely. It's a long way off. I can just see it. Looks all wrapped up like a...a mummy."

"A mummy! That's weird. That's just what I was thinking this morning when I got out of bed and looked out the—"

"...*I'm Rick Phillips for Radio 1360, your information center for this storm.*"

Something in the tone of the announcer's voice had stopped Jamie. The voice sounded, well...different.

"Kevin?"

"Mmm?"

"That guy on the radio—did you think he sounded kind of strange?"

"I guess I wasn't paying much attention to him. I was looking at the snow. It kind of hypnotizes you, you know?"

Somehow Kevin seemed different now, more serious. Jamie had never known Kevin to be serious about anything. The music that had been playing on the radio stopped, and the voice was back.

"*Time now is 8:25, and that snow just keeps coming down. And do we have some new cancellations for you!*"

The wind outside moaned and shifted the snow in crazy patterns. That voice *was* different, and Jamie didn't like the way it sounded. It was—what? A little like some kind of cartoon-character villain, sort of half-mocking like. Sort of...unreal.

"Hey, you're right," he heard Kevin say. "That voice sounds—"

"Shh, listen."

"Here's the big one, friends. Listen carefully." He pronounced carefully the way Bela Lugosi might say it in a Dracula movie, drawing out the *a-a-r* sound with a special menace. *"Here it is. Merrimack Valley Mill is cancelled."* The radio went immediately to music again, some goofy love song.

For a long while, neither boy spoke. Finally, Kevin broke the silence. "Jamie?"

"I'm here."

"Jamie, I'm lookin' out the window, and somethin' looks funny."

"What do you mean, something looks funny?"

Kevin waited a long time before answering. "This isn't right. I can see Pennacock Park."

"So? You can see practically everything in the city from your apartment."

"Yeah, but not the park. I never could see it before."

"Aw, c'mon, Kevin, it's as big as a football field. Bigger. You must have seen it."

"No, no, I'm tellin' you Jamie, I never could see it before. The mill was always in the way. Oh, no!"

Jamie heard Kevin draw in a shocked-sounding breath. "What?" Jamie asked.

"I can see the park because the mill isn't there."

Jamie laughed, but the laugh came out a little hollow. "Give me a break, Kevin. Of course the mill is there. You're talking goofy, dufus."

Kevin sounded angry. "Look, Jamie, I oughta know where that mill is from my own window, and I'm tellin' you it disappeared. That's why I can see the park, because the mill ain't hidin' it anymore."

Outside Jamie's window, the wind whooped up into a howl and threw snow against the pane. "Kevin, what are you saying? My dad works there."

"I know," Kevin said quietly. "So does mine."

"...at 8:39, this is Radio 1360, your Voice of the Storm." The voice had that mocking, Dracula tone again, more so than before. *"And in case you thought we were through with cancellations, consider this one, my friends. This just in—Sanborn's in Merrimack. Sanborn's has been cancelled."*

Immediately there was more music.

"Kevin?"

"I'm here."

"Kevin, my mom works at Sanborn's."

"I know."

"Kevin, can you see Sanborn's?"

After a moment, Kevin replied, "I can't tell, there's so much snow."

"Kevin, look, I'm going to hang up for a minute. I'll call you back."

"Promise?"

"Promise." Jamie clicked down the receiver. Then, after a pause, he punched out the familiar digits of Sanborn's, digits he had used so many times before to call his mother when he had a question or a problem. As he looked up from the phone, his eye caught the photo on his mother's bureau—his mom, his dad, and himself smiling in the sun on summer vacation two years ago. Somehow he felt oddly moved by the photo and other familiar objects placed on the bureau.

He listened for the phone to ring at Sanborn's, straining to hear that soft burring sound. He heard only a blank hissing on the line and the murmuring of the wind outside, where, he could see, the snow was falling harder than ever. Finally he gave up and dialed Kevin back. Kevin answered before the first ring was finished, "Jamie?"

"Yeah, it's me. Look, I tried to call my mom, but there's no answer at Sanborn's. It doesn't even ring. So maybe the telephone lines are down. That sometimes happens in a snowstorm, right? I mean, you ought to know. You've lived through other snowstorms before, right?" Jamie realized he was speaking rapidly, nervously, but he couldn't help it.

"*. . . We hope you're staying tuned, because we're having more snow cancellations. Exotron Technologies has been can-*

celled. *Compton Industries has been cancelled. Pennacock Mall has been cancelled.*"

"Jamie!" Jamie had never heard Kevin's voice sound the way it did now.

"Your mom works at Pennacock Mall, doesn't she?"

"Jamie—there's something awful wrong. The downtown, out my window. There's, like, parts of it gone. I mean, really gone. Like holes in it."

"OK, maybe it's a mirage. Sometimes in the desert, you know, the heat waves coming up from the ground and all make things blurry and wavy and you think you see things...."

"Shh. Jamie, listen. The radio!"

"*... and still more Storm Center Radio updates for you. Ready for this one?*" The voice sounded thick, gloating, dreadful. "*Reeds Ferry Apartments, in Merrimack, cancelled.*" Music. Some woman was singing, "Let it snow, let it snow, let it snow."

A brittle finger of ice wormed its way up Jamie's spine. Kevin lived in the Reeds Ferry Apartments complex. Jamie swallowed hard to get his voice back.

"Kevin?"

Nothing.

"Kevin? This isn't funny, anymore. You're just trying to scare me." Jamie laughed nervously. "So, OK, you win. You scared me. Now stop it!"

Nothing.

"Kevin!!!"

Nothing on the line at all but a dead, dry hissing, like the sound that might come out of the grinning and remorseless mouth of a reptile.

"Kevin, please be there. *Please!*"

Silence. Silence on the phone, and the radio crooning softly along, unconcerned.

Jamie hung up the phone and sat looking at the snow, which had grown into a nightmare of whiteness pressing at the window, blotting out everything, tumbling and turning and writhing in the madness of the wind.

He looked at the photo of himself and his parents smiling in the Arizona sun. Quickly, he jumped from the bed and ran to grab the frame. He glanced out of the window. Everything was wrapped in white. He could see nothing, not the woods beyond the backyard, not the bird feeder outside the window, not the driveway—nothing. Jamie dashed back to the mattress. Pulling the sheets closer around him and pressing the photo to his cheek, he waited for the music to end.

THE RUUM

by Arthur Porges

*The animals were paralyzed, preserved as
living specimens. Now the ruum intended
on preserving one more—a human.*

Then: The cruiser *Ilkor* had just passed beyond the
orbit of Pluto when a worried officer reported to the
Commander.

"I regret to inform you, sir," he said nervously, "that a
Type H-9 Ruum has been left behind on the third planet,
together with anything it may have collected."

The Commander's three eyes turned from green to
blue, but her voice remained level.

"How was the ruum set?"

"For a maximum radius of 30 miles, and 160 pounds,
plus or minus 15."

The Commander was silent for several seconds. Then
she said, "We cannot change course now. We will retrieve

the ruum on our return in a few weeks. In the meantime, confine the person responsible to quarters."

But at the end of its outward run, the cruiser met an enemy raider. When the battle was over, both ships, radioactive and loaded with dead, began a billion-year orbit around the star.

And on Earth, it was the age of the dinosaurs.

☠

Now: When the two men had unloaded the supplies, Jim Irwin watched his partner climb into the little plane with pontoons.

"Don't forget to mail that letter to my wife," Jim shouted.

"The minute I land," Walt Leonard called back. "And you find some uranium. Make us millionaires. And don't rub noses with any grizzlies."

Jim thumbed his nose as the plane skimmed across the lake and rose into the sky. Suddenly he felt a strange chill. For three weeks he would be alone in this remote valley of the Canadian Rockies. If anything happened, he would be completely on his own until Walt returned. And if there was any uranium in the valley, he had to find it in twenty-one days.

To work then—and no gloomy thoughts. With the unhurried skills of a trained woodsman, he built a lean-

☠

to in the shelter of a rocky overhang. He piled his supplies back under the ledge, covered by a tarp and protected from animal prowlers. All but the dynamite—he hid that carefully two hundred yards away.

The first two weeks went by swiftly but with no finds. Only one good area remained, and just enough time to explore it. Early one morning Jim set off for the northeast part of the valley.

He took the Geiger counter and his rifle. The .30-06 was a nuisance, but huge grizzlies have touchy tempers and take a lot of killing. The .22 pistol he left in his holster in the lean-to.

Jim walked all morning, sometimes feeling a burst of hope as the counter began to chatter. But its sputter always died down. Apparently, he and Walt had picked the wrong valley. Jim's cheerfulness faded.

He decided to think about his lunch. The sun, as well as his stomach, said it was time. He had just prepared to fish a foaming brook, when he rounded a grassy knoll and came across a sight that made him stiffen to a halt.

The scene was like some giant outdoor butcher shop. A wide variety of animals, neatly lined up in threes, stretched almost as far as the eye could see. Those nearest him were ordinary deer, bear, cougar, and mountain sheep. But down the line were many strange beasts. One near the extreme end he recognized at once. There had been a specimen like it in the museum at home.

No doubt about it—the body was that of a stegosaur, no bigger than a pony.

Fascinated, Jim walked down the lines. Glancing at one lizard, he saw an eye flutter. Then it came to him—the animals were not dead but paralyzed and somehow preserved. *Still alive?* Perspiration prickled Jim's forehead. *A stegosaur still alive after 150 million years?*

All at once he noticed something else. The victims were roughly the same size. Nowhere was there a really large animal. No tyrannosaur. No mammoth. Each specimen was about the size of a large sheep. He was puzzling this out, when the underbrush rustled behind him.

☠

For a second, Jim wondered if a blob of mercury had rolled into the clearing. The rounded object moved with just such a liquid motion. It whipped out and retracted a number of metal rods with lens-like structures at their tips. The object rolled steadily toward him at about five miles per hour. From its look, Jim had no doubt that it meant to add him to the heap of living-dead specimens.

He sprang back a number of spaces, unslinging his rifle. A grim smile touched his lips as he pulled the trigger. He knew what one of those 180-grain slugs could do at 2,700 feet per second.

☠

Wham. The familiar kick against his shoulder. *E-e-e-e-!* The whining screech of a ricochet. He sucked in his breath. At a mere twenty yards, the bullet had bounced off the ruum.

Quickly, Jim blasted two more rounds. The ruum kept coming. When it was six feet away, he saw a gleaming hook flick out and a stinglike probe waiting between them. The stinger dripped green liquid.

Jim ran.

He weighed exactly 149 pounds—light, trim, and fit. He had no trouble pulling ahead. The ruum seemed unable to increase its speed. But Jim felt no relief on that score. No animal on Earth could keep a steady five-mile-per-hour pace forever.

As he ran, Jim began to shed all surplus material. He hesitated over the rifle, but military training impelled him to keep the weapon. The Geiger counter he placed gently on a flat rock while barely breaking his stride.

One thing was certain. This would be a fighting retreat. He'd use every survival trick he learned in his hazard-filled lifetime. Whatever that thing was, wherever it had come from, it would find him no easy prey.

Taking deep, measured breaths, he loped along, looking with shrewd eyes for anything that might be used to his advantage in this weird contest. Suddenly he came upon a sight that made him pause. It was a point where a huge boulder overhung the trail. He grinned as he remembered a Malay mantrap that had once saved his life.

Purposely dragging his feet, he made a clear trail directly under the boulder. Then he walked backward in his own prints and jumped up to a point behind the balanced rock.

After digging under it with his belt knife and ramming it with his shoulder, he felt it teeter. He was crouching there, panting, when the ruum rolled over the hill.

Seemingly intent on the footprints, the alien sphere rippled along directly under the boulder. As it did so, Jim gave a savage shout and, thrusting with his whole weight against the boulder, toppled it directly on the machine below. Five tons of snow fell from a height of twelve feet.

After another shout, this time of triumph, Jim scrambled down to the trail. He stared at the huge boulder, shaking his head dazedly. Then he gave the solid rock a kick in celebration of his victory. "Take that, you bloody butcher," he said out loud.

Then he leaped back, his eyes wild. The giant rock was shifting. Even as he stared, part of a gray form appeared under the nearest edge, somehow working its way loose from the tons of weight. With a choked cry, Jim turned and resumed his flight.

He ran hard a full mile down the trail. Looking back, he could just make out a dark dot moving away from the boulder. He sat down and put his head in his hands. What now?

He forced himself to relax and nibbled some dried beef, biscuits, and chocolate. A few sips of water, and he felt ready to resume the struggle.

☠

After running fifteen minutes, he came to a sheer face of rock about thirty feet high. If he could make it to the top of that rock, the ruum would have to detour and might lose the trail.

He looked at the sun. Huge and crimson, it was almost touching the western horizon. He would have to move fast before darkness came. Using every crack and tiny ledge, he fought his way up the cliff. He had just reached the top when the ruum rolled up to the base of the wall of rock. But the machine did not detour. It hesitated for only a few seconds. Then it began to send out metallic wands. One of these, topped with lenses, waved in the air. Jim drew back too late—their unblinking gaze had spotted him peering down.

Immediately, all the wands retracted, and a slender rod began to shoot straight up toward him. As he watched, its barbed tip gripped the cliff almost under his nose.

Jim leaped to his feet. Already the rod was shortening as the ruum swallowed it, pulling itself up along the slender

☠

metal track. Seizing a length of dry branch and inserting one end under the hook, Jim began to pry.

There was a flash, and Jim felt a surge of power that shattered the end of the branch. He dropped it with a gasp of pain and backed off several yards, full of rage. Snarling, he unslung his rifle. Now he had the ruum where he wanted it.

Kneeling to steady his aim, Jim sighted at the hook and fired. The hook disappeared in an explosion of rock and dust, and there was a soggy thud at the base of the cliff. Jim shouted with relief and joy. Not only had the heavy slug blasted the metal claw loose, it had also smashed a big gap in the cliff's edge. The ruum would have a hard time using that part of the cliff again.

Jim looked down and saw a gray form at the bottom. He grinned. Every time the ruum clamped a hook over the bluff, he'd blow the hook loose. He had plenty of ammunition. Sooner or later that devilish machine would have to accept a detour.

Then he looked again. Down below, the squat machine was sending up three rods at the same time. The rods snagged the cliff's edge at intervals of about four feet.

Jim whipped the rifle to his shoulder. The first shot was a bulls-eye, knocking loose the left-hand hook. His second shot knocked off the center barb. But even as he whirled to level at number three, he saw it was hopeless.

The first hook was back in place. No matter how well he shot, one rod would always be pulling the ruum to the top.

☠

Jim hung the rifle muzzle down from a small tree and ran into the deepening dark. All those years he had spent to toughen his body were paying off now. But so what? What could he do? Was there anything that would stop the infernal machine behind him?

The he remembered the dynamite.

Gradually he changed his course back toward his camp by the lake. Overhead, the stars brightened, pointing the way. At times he stopped to rest or to check his direction. But he could never rest long before the sound of the ruum came to his ears.

Shortly after sunrise he reached the lake and his camp. He staggered from exhaustion and his eyes closed. He struck himself feebly on the nose, popping his eyes open. There was the dynamite. The sight of those greasy sticks snapped him wide awake.

He forced himself to stay calm and to think carefully. The dynamite must be set off from a distance at the very moment the ruum passed over it. He couldn't use a fuse—the rate of burning wasn't constant enough to allow precise timing. Sweat poured down his face. He had to think of an answer, but he was so tired, so tired. His

☠

head drooped. He snapped it up—and saw the .22 where he had left it in the lean-to.

His sunken eyes flashed.

Moving with frantic haste, he piled all the percussion caps along the dynamite sticks. Then, staggering out to his trail, he carefully placed the box about twenty yards from a rocky ledge.

Jim had scarcely hunched down behind the ledge when his tireless pursuer appeared five hundred yards away. He slid into a crack where he could aim at the dynamite and still be shielded from the blast. If it was a shield...when all those sticks blew up at only twenty yards.

☠

Suddenly he was in full awareness. A huge form had come along the edge of the lake and was sniffing at the explosive. Of all the times for a grizzly to be snooping about! It had the whole camp to explore. Why did it have to choose the dynamite? Just a touch could blow one of the percussion caps. And then....

The grizzly heard a noise and raised its massive head to stare at the strange object approaching. Jim snickered. Until he had met the ruum, the giant North American grizzly was the only thing in the world he had feared. And now the two terrors of his life were meeting head-on— and he was laughing.

☠

About six feet from the bear the ruum paused. The grizzly reared with a ferocious growl, terrible teeth flashing white against red lips. The ruum started to roll past, still intent on its specimen. The bear closed in, roaring, and gave the ruum a hard swat with one mighty paw armed with razor-sharp claws. The blow would have ripped apart a rhinoceros. Dust flew from the machine, and it was knocked back several inches. It paused, then rippled on, ignoring the bear.

The lord of the woods wasn't settling for a draw. With incredible speed it pulled the ruum to its chest with shaggy forearms and clamped its jaws on the gray surface. Jim half rose. "Get it!" he croaked.

Then silver metal gleamed bright against the gray. There was a flash, swift and deadly. The roar of the king became a gurgle, and its one-ton bulk fell to the ground. Blood poured from its slashed throat as it died.

And the ruum rolled past the giant corpse, still intent on the man's trail. "OK, baby," Jim said under his breath, "come and get it." And very calmly he squeezed the trigger of his pistol.

Sound first. Then giant hands lifted his body from where he lay and let him go. He came down hard in a patch of nettles. But he didn't care. He noticed that the birds were silent. Then there was a fluid thump as something heavy struck the ground a few feet away. Then all was quiet.

Jim lifted his head. He saw an enormous smoking crater in the earth. He also saw, gray-white now from powdered rock, the ruum.

The machine was under a handsome pine tree. Even as Jim watched, wondering if the ringing in his ears would ever go away, the machine began to roll toward him.

He fumbled for his pistol. It was gone. It had dropped somewhere out of reach. He wanted to pray but couldn't get his brain to focus....

The ruum was a foot away now, and Jim closed his eyes. He felt cool, metallic fingers touch, grip, lift. His body was raised several inches and juggled oddly. Helpless but strangely serene, he waited for the stinger with the green liquid. He thought of the lizard with the trembling eye and wondered what it would be like to lie paralyzed but mentally aware for a million years.

Then, gently, the ruum put him back on the ground. When he opened his eyes some seconds later, the sphere was rolling away. Watching it go released a flood of emotions, and he began to sob softly. It seemed only a matter of moments before he heard the seaplane's engine and opened his eyes to see Walt Leonard peering down at him.

☠

Later, in the plane, Walt grinned suddenly and said: "Well, no uranium, but we'll do OK. I can get a heli-

☠

copter, a big one. We'll pick up some of those prehistoric specimens, and museums will pay us plenty."

Jim shook his head. "What about that robot keeping watch on its collection?"

"It can't fly, can it?"

"Who knows?' Jim responded. "I wouldn't bet on it."

"Well, maybe we can work out some rig that will let us retrieve the bodies from the air. Maybe grab the robot too."

"No way," said Jim. "I'm through messing with that thing." He paused, "All that running I did, and then the stupid thing didn't want me at all."

"Yeah," Walt said, "that was really weird. And after that marathon. I admire your guts, man." He glanced sideways at Jim Irwin's haggard face. "That run cost you plenty. I figure you lost over ten pounds."

PART II
LACHESIS, WEAVER
OF GOOD AND EVIL

A MEETING WITH DEATH

Adapted from the "Pardoner's Tale" from
The Canterbury Tales
by Geoffrey Chaucer

*They were rakes, rascals, scoundrels—all three.
But they had made a pact. Together they
would seek out death and destroy him.*

During the 1300s, a terrible pestilence swept across Asia
and Europe claiming hundreds of thousands of victims.
Some people called the dreadful disease the Plague. Others
called it the Black Death. No one knew the cause of the dying
or from where the pestilence had come. No one then understood how the Black Death could steal so silently, so swiftly
from one village to the next. In fear, some people fled their
homes to seek a safer place. Others remained behind to con-
front, perhaps even to defeat, the deadly specter. The setting

of the story that follows is a rural village in England, a village in which Death walks boldly among the people.

☠

Early one morning, before the church bells have rung to announce the start of day, three young men gather in a tavern. They are dressed as gentlemen, but their drunken behavior gives away their true nature. They are rakes, rascals, scoundrels—all three.

This morning they have come not to feed their empty bellies, but to quench their thirst for more wine. A skinny boy, whose mother is the tavern keeper, sets another jug of wine on their table. Suddenly from outside comes the low and mournful bong of a funeral bell. Villagers file past the tavern door, carrying a corpse on a stretcher. The first rascal wipes the wine from his lips and goes to the door to watch. "Do you see this?" Oswald calls to his companions. "A funeral starts our day."

"You, boy!" shouts Roland, the second rascal. "Go quickly and ask whose corpse this is that passes by here."

"And look to it that you report his name correctly," adds John, the third rake in the group.

"But, sirs, there is no need for that," the boy answers. "It was told to me two hours before you came in here. The dead man was an old companion of yours."

"A friend of ours? Tell us the name!"

☠

"I don't know his name, only that I have seen him here with you. Last night he was sitting on that very bench when suddenly there came a thief who, with a spear, smote the man's heart in two." The boy demonstrates by thrusting a make-believe sword forward. "Then, just as quickly, the thief went away without a word."

"A thief?" says Oswald, turning from the door and looking at the other rakes. "Who is this vile creature?"

"The people call the thief Death."

"Death! Ha!" Roland scoffs and reaches for the jug to pour himself more wine. "The stupid boy spins tales to tease us."

Marie, the boy's mother, has been listening and now she steps forward. "The child speaks the truth. Death has slain both man and woman, child and laborer in a large village over a mile hence. I believe Death must live there."

"If I were you," the boy tells the rakes, "I'd take care or Death will do you harm too."

Roland mocks him. "Do *us* harm! Now the boy thinks he can frighten us."

"I would not laugh if I were you," warns Marie. "A thousand people, I tell you, have died!"

Roland pushes back his stool and stands, made bold by the liquid courage of the wine he has drunk. "I vow by holy bones to seek out this mad creature. I shall seek Death on the highways and byways!" He turns to his two companions and challenges them. "Listen, my friends. We three are all of one mind. Let each of us hold up his hand to the other two and each of us become the others' brother, and we will slay this traitor, this thief Death."

Oswald glances anxiously at the open tavern door. The mournful sounds of the funeral bell still echo along the street outside.

"Well? Are we brothers?" Roland presses. "Do we pledge our word of honor to live and die for each other? Together we can defeat Death!" He holds out his hand.

John hesitates, then he leaps to his feet and clasps Roland's hand. "Yes! Death shall be slain!"

The two rascals look at Oswald. "The thief who has slain so many, on my honor, will be slain before night falls." He steps to the table and places his hand on theirs. "Brothers."

The pact made, the three rakes storm from the tavern into the morning sun.

☠

Because Marie has said that Death lives in the neighboring village, the three rakes head in that direction. They go not quite a half mile when they come upon an old woman on the road. A dirty cloth is wrapped about her head and shoulders. Her face is pale and withered; her fingers, bony and twisted with age.

☠

"Good morrow, lords," she greets in a voice as old and brittle as bone. "May the saints protect you."

"Bad cess to you, old woman!" Roland says with a grimace. "Why are you all wrapped up except for your face?"

"Yes," says Oswald. "Why do you live so long, in such old age?"

The old woman uses a twisted branch for a cane. She leans upon it and gazes into Oswald's face. "Because even if I walked to India I could not find a man either in a city or in a village who would exchange his youth for my age. Therefore, I must keep my age for as long as I live."

"She's making up riddles, I think," laughs John.

"Move out of our way, you old crone," barks Roland. "Your old bag of a body takes up too much of the road."

"It is wrong of you to speak rudely to an old woman," she whines. "Have I injured you by word or deed?"

"*You* injure us? That's a howl!" All three rascals laugh.

"I warn you," says the crackling voice. "Do no harm to an old woman any more than you would wish others to do to you in your old age—*if* you live till then."

"Leave her be. Her mind is as old as her body, and she makes no sense."

Roland shoves her aside, and the three rakes walk on.

"Not even Death will take my life," says the old woman. "And so I walk like a restless prisoner. Lo! How I fade away, flesh and blood and skin!"

Roland turns. "Death you say? You have seen Death?"

The old woman mumbles to herself, "Oh, when shall my old bones be at rest? I am cursed to wander from village to village. I must go where I have to go."

Roland grabs the old woman's thin arm. "You spoke just now of this traitor Death, who slays all our friends in this country. Where is Death? Tell us! Or you shall pay for it!"

John peers closely at her wrinkled face. "Perhaps she is Death's spy. Finding young lives for Death to snatch away!"

With eyes dark and clouded, the old woman stares without fear into their arrogant faces. "Well, sirs, if you are so eager to find Death, then turn up this crooked path. By my faith, I left him there in that grove, under a tree, and there he will stay."

"We mean to slay him for all the young people whose lives he has stolen," Oswald says. "What do you think of that, you old crone?"

Her blistered lips crack into a thin smile. "Your boasting won't make him hide himself at all. Death is not afraid of rascals like you. Do you see that large oak? You shall find him there, waiting for you."

Roland lets go of her arm. At once, the three rakes turn and run along the crooked path.

☠

"Is this the tree?" Roland cries. "But I see no one!"

The three rakes stand before the large oak, looking now up into its branches, looking now through the surrounding shadows for Death.

"The old crone has tricked us," says John. "I told you she spoke in riddles."

"Here! What's this?" cries Oswald. Partially hidden in the tangle of grass and thorns at the base of the oak tree is a large sack. Oswald frees it and unties the rope around its closed neck. "Why it's gold!" he gasps. "GOLD!"

"Let me see!" Roland grabs the bag from Oswald and spills some of the coins into his palm. They fall in a glittering stream to the ground. John quickly scoops the fallen coins into his own hands.

"It *is* gold!" cries John. "Two hundred pieces of gold at least!"

"We're rich!" laughs Oswald. "Rich!"

The three hoot wildly with joy. Already they have forgotten their pledge to find and slay Death.

"What shall we do? How shall we divide it?" asks John.

The three sit on the ground with the sack of gold in the center.

Roland speaks first. "Brothers, pay attention to what I have to say. Fortune has given us this treasure so that we can live our lives in mirth and jollity. As lightly as it came, so we shall spend it!"

"Who would have guessed that we should have such

good luck today!" muses Oswald. "A day that began with a funeral! Let's take it now and go."

"Not so quick!" warns Roland. "Think but a minute. If we carry this gold from this hidden place to my house—"

"*Your* house?" interrupts John.

"Or else to yours," Roland quickly adds, "Someone will see us. They will think us thieves and hang us for our treasure."

"Yes, yes," agrees John. "We cannot carry the gold to our homes in the daylight."

"We shall draw lots to see who among us will return to the village and secretly bring back food and wine," suggests Roland. "One shall go and two shall remain here to guard the treasure."

The three rascals look at one another. Once more Roland holds out his hand to make a pact. And once more first John, then Oswald, agree to the deal. Roland draws three straws from his pocket, snaps off the end of one, then holds all three in his fist. John draws first. Then Oswald picks. At the same time, each rake opens his hand. Oswald's straw is the shortest, but he does not leave at once. "We are brothers?" he asks.

"We made a pledge, didn't we?"

"And you will wait for me here?" Oswald asks, still unsure.

"Yes, yes!" says John. "We shall wait for you here. Do

you think I would let *him*," he nods to Roland, "get away with our shares of the gold?"

Oswald hurries away, back down the crooked path. No sooner is he out of sight when Roland leans closer to John. "It is a great deal of gold."

"Yes, indeed it is."

"It would be greater if divided by two instead of three," suggests Roland.

John grins. "What are you thinking?"

"That two are stronger than one."

Roland cups the coins and lets them fall, glittering from his hand into John's. John stares at the golden pool in his palm.

"Yes," says John, "two *are* stronger than one."

☠

As Oswald hurries back to the village, he imagines gold falling like yellow sunshine from Roland's hand to the ground. Why, he wonders, should he share it? After all, he was the one who discovered the happy sack. *If I should have it all*, he thinks as he nears the village, *why I'd be the happiest man alive!*

In the village, he spies an apothecary shop, where herbs and medicines of all kinds—poisons too—are sold. He doesn't hesitate, but enters the shop at once. "I have a problem," he tells the apothecary.

☠

"What problem is that?"

"Rats," Oswald answers at once. "Many rats. Under my house. And a polecat too. The beast has been killing my chickens."

"I have just the thing you need. No creature in all this world, if it eats or drinks of this mixture, will not lose its life at once." He hands Oswald a glass jar.

"Are you certain of this? It must work quickly, very quickly."

"Oh, yes. The rats shall die in less time than it would take you to take ten steps."

The young rake pays for his poison, then hurries to another shop and buys three skins of wine. Carefully, he pours the poison into two of the skins, then makes a small mark on the third. Smiling slyly, he raises the skins. "To your health, dear friends."

Quite pleased with himself, Oswald returns to the tavern to order some food. The tavern owner recognizes him. "Ah, it is you. Have you found Death?"

"Don't be foolish. Why should I want to find Death?" Oswald asks. "That was only a boasting game we played hours ago."

"Where are your two companions?"

"Gone. As far away from this village as they can get. They shall not return."

Marie gives the young man bread and cheese, and he

hurries away, heading back toward the grove of trees and the gold that awaits him.

☠

John stands and points down the crooked road. "I see him. He is coming."

"Remember our plan," Roland says. "Do not betray me."

Oswald returns and sets the skins of wine in the grass. Although seeming to do so casually, he makes sure that the marked skin is the one nearest him. Roland reaches hungrily for a crust of bread. Oswald watches as John picks up the skin nearest him. He raises it to his lip, then hesitates. "What took you so long?" he asks suspiciously.

"That foolish woman in the tavern wanted to know if we had found Death." Oswald grins. "I told her it was a game we were playing, that we had better things to do. It is not our worry where Death may go."

"A game. That's right," says Roland, his mouth full of cheese. "Death may come and go as he pleases. It is no skin off our backsides, is it?" He laughs and John laughs, as well. Soon all three rakes are slapping their knees and hugging their sides.

Then suddenly, John lunges at Oswald, pinning him to the ground. "Here is another game to play, brother." In a flash, Roland pulls out his knife and plunges it into

☠

Oswald's heart. Oswald's struggle lasts but a few moments, and then he is still.

John and Roland sit back, stunned at what they have done. The air around them seems to hold its breath. And then Roland laughs in triumph. "It is done. The gold is ours. Come, let us celebrate."

"What about—" John nods toward the body.

"What about him? It was his misfortune to draw the shortest straw. We'll bury him later. But first," Roland holds up a skin of wine, "we drink. To our fortune!"

John brings his own skin of wine to his lips. "To long and idle lives," he toasts.

Each man throws back his head and drinks.

The apothecary's words are true. The poison is violent, strong, and quick. So quick, in fact, that when the old woman steps from the shadows of the grove to retrieve her gold, the three rakes offer no resistance at all. How can they? They are as silent and unmoving as the tree trunks that surround them.

"You think you can defeat Death?" she asks the scoundrels who stare back at her with unblinking eyes. "It cannot be done. Your greed was the poison that killed you. May someone bury your flesh before it rots in the sun."

And with that, Death shuffles away.

THE BIRTHMARK

by Nathaniel Hawthorne

*The birthmark was nature's flaw. But what
nature could not perfect, science could.*

Aylmer gazed unhappily at his wife, Georgiana, across the room. She was beautiful, except for a small birthmark on her cheek. Aylmer was a scientist, not a doctor, and before his marriage to Georgiana, he had scarcely noticed the mark. But for weeks now it had been troubling him. It was like a stain upon white marble. He had begun to hate it.

"My dear," he ventured one day, "has it ever occurred to you that the mark upon your cheek could be removed?" he asked.

Georgiana smiled uneasily. "It is so faint, I often forget it is even there. To tell you the truth, it has been so often called a charm that I was simple enough to imagine it might be so."

"Upon another face perhaps it might," replied her husband. "But never on yours. I find it shocking!"

Georgiana was alarmed. "Shocking?" she cried, deeply hurt; at first reddening with momentary anger, but then bursting into tears. "Then why did you take me from my mother's side? You cannot love what shocks you!"

The singular mark was deeply interwoven with the texture and substance of her face. In the usual state of her complexion—a healthy though delicate bloom—the mark wore a tint of deeper crimson, which imperfectly defined its shape amid the surrounding rosiness. When she blushed it gradually became more indistinct, and finally vanished amid the triumphant rush of blood that bathed the whole cheek with its brilliant glow. But if any shifting motion caused her to turn pale, there was the mark again. Although quite small, its shape bore a similarity to the human hand.

Aylmer stood, agitated now. The birthmark was a fatal flaw of nature. "If it were not for the mark, you would be perfect!"

Georgiana turned away, and Aylmer was left brooding. He was a scientist. He had spent his entire life in his laboratory working on perfecting what nature could not. A simple birthmark was a small thing compared to the larger experiments with which he was concerned. But he said nothing more.

Day after day, whenever she looked up, Georgiana found Aylmer staring at her, sometimes with a sour expression, other times with a look of appalled disgust. Georgiana soon learned to shudder at his gaze. A glance from him would change the roses of her cheeks into a deathlike paleness, amid which the crimson hand was brought out strongly. Soon, she too began to hate the sight of the mark.

Late one night, when the lights were growing dim so as hardly to betray the stain on the poor wife's cheek, she herself, for the first time, voluntarily took up the subject.

"Do you remember, my dear Aylmer," said she, with a feeble attempt at a smile, "having a dream last night about this odious birthmark?"

"None! None whatever!" replied Aylmer, startled that somehow his wife had read his nightmare. But then he added, in a dry, cold tone, trying not to betray his emotion, "I might have dreamed of it. Perhaps I did, for I have thought of the mark often before I fall asleep."

"You *did* dream of it!" she pressed. "And it was a terrible dream! I wonder that you can forget it. I heard you speaking in your sleep. You cried out, 'It is in her heart now; we must have it out!' Do you not remember the dream now?"

Indeed he did remember. It was very clear to him. He was in his laboratory, and he was pressing the blade of a knife into the soft skin of Georgiana's cheek. The deeper he cut, the deeper the birthmark sank. He could not get to the root of it. Aylmer had wakened in a cold sweat. Beside him, Georgiana was sleeping peacefully. The mark was still there, as grotesque to him as ever.

"Aylmer," resumed Georgiana, solemnly, "I know not what may be the cost to both of us to rid me of this fatal birthmark. Perhaps its removal may cause cureless deformity; or it may be the stain goes as deep as life itself. But let the attempt be made. You have learned science. Cannot you remove this little, little mark, which I cover with the tips of two small fingers? Is this beyond your power? To do so would give you peace and save your poor wife from madness."

Aylmer beamed. "Noblest, dearest, tenderest wife," he cried, "doubt not my power. I have already given this matter the deepest thought. I feel fully competent to remove the mark without error or danger to you. I shall make you perfect!"

Aylmer kissed his wife's cheek—her unblemished cheek. "No one will equal your beauty," he promised.

"Is that so important to you, Aylmer?" Georgiana asked, sadness in her voice.

"Your happiness is what is important to me," he answered. "And you have just admitted that you are dreadfully unhappy knowing how the mark disturbs me."

And that, of course, was quite true.

The dream he had dreamt was only foolishness. Aylmer had no intention of removing the birthmark by an operation. He had a different method, a chemical solution. For days, then weeks, he worked in his laboratory until at last he had discovered the right combination of chemicals. With the liquid mixed and ready, Aylmer drew his wife into the laboratory.

As she stepped over the threshold, Georgiana was cold and tremulous. Aylmer looked cheerfully into her pale face, with intent to reassure her, but was so startled with the intense glow of the birthmark that he shuddered violently. His wife fainted.

Quickly, he lifted her and carried her into a private room where he sometimes slept and studied. When Georgiana recovered consciousness she found herself breathing a sweet, penetrating fragrance. "Where am I? Ah, I remember," she said, faintly, and she placed her hand over her cheek to hide the terrible mark from her husband's eyes.

The scene around her looked like enchantment. Aylmer had converted the smoky, dingy, somber room into a beautiful apartment. The walls were hung with gorgeous curtains, which fell from ceiling to floor and shut out all light that might interfere with his chemical experimentations. Perfumed lamps emitted flames of various hues—blues, corals, pale greens—uniting in a soft radiance.

He told her he had been working to perfect a liquid to prolong life for years, perhaps forever. "Death is the ultimate flaw of nature, is it not? One day I shall discover an elixir of life that will bring man immortality," he said enthusiastically.

"Aylmer, are you in earnest? It is terrible to possess such power, or even to dream of possessing it."

"Do not tremble, my love," said her husband. "I would not wrong either you or myself with my experiments. I mean to improve the world."

Georgiana loved her husband, despite his aversion to the mark upon her cheek. But she felt sorry for him, as well. For a man of science who dreams of perfecting nature can never be satisfied. He is doomed to fail even if the experiment succeeds.

Aylmer bid her to follow him into the laboratory. In comparison to the boudoir, the laboratory was a gray room of brick. The furnace, hot and feverish, caught her eye. Quantities of soot clustered above it and seemed to have been burning for ages. Around the room were glass tubes, cylinders, crucibles, and other apparatus of chemical research. The room seemed naked after the elegance and sweet perfume of the boudoir. Aylmer, too, seemed more serious, more pale, as if the laboratory's gaseous odors were seeping inside his soul.

"Behold," Aylmer said, and he held up a vial of silver

liquid. On the table stood a geranium diseased with yellow blotches which had overspread all its leaves. Georgiana watched as Aylmer poured a small quantity of the liquid upon the soil in which it grew. In a little time, when the roots of the plant had taken up the moisture, the unsightly blotches began to be extinguished as new, green tips of vegetation began to sprout and uncurl. Within minutes, the geranium was lush and green, a perfect plant again. Crimson blooms crowned its head.

"Why, it is magical!" Georgiana cried.

"No, it is not magic," Aylmer said. "I am not a sorcerer with a book of spells and potions. I am a scientist. That is why you must trust me, my dear."

"Will you put this silver liquid on my face?" she asked.

"Oh, no. The mark runs too deep beneath the skin. You must drink the liquid. Unless science deceives me," he told her, "it will not fail."

"I submit," she replied, calmly. "I will quaff whatever draught you bring me; but it will be on the same principle that would induce me to take a dose of poison if offered by your hand."

"My dear wife," said Aylmer, deeply moved. "I knew not the height and depth of your nature until now. But why do you speak of poison, of dying? The liquid cannot fail. There is no danger. I have tested it. The strength of the potion is right."

"Danger? There is but one danger—that this horrible stigma shall be left upon my cheek and I shall go mad!" she cried. "Give me the goblet."

"Drink then," exclaimed Aylmer, with admiration for his wife, "and you shall be perfect."

She quaffed the liquid and returned the goblet to his hand.

"I am grateful," she said. "Now, dearest, let me sleep. My senses are closing over my spirit like the leaves around the heart of a rose at sunset."

She spoke the last words with a gentle reluctance, as if it required almost more energy than she could command to pronounce the syllables. Scarcely had they loitered through her lips when she was lost in slumber.

Aylmer sat by her side, watching her closely. Not the minutest symptom escaped him. Her cheeks flushed; her eyelids quivered. Each tiny detail he recorded in his notebook. So engrossed was he in the progress of the operation that he failed to notice that the geranium on the table had begun to droop. The bloom's crimson petals drifted silently to the table top.

With each breath in and each breath out, the outline of the crimson hand upon Georgiana's cheek became less noticeable. She stirred in her deep sleep and murmured, then sighed, and the mark faded even more. Aylmer scribbled another note. When he looked up again, he was jubilant.

"By Heaven! It is gone!" said Aylmer. "I can scarcely trace it now. Success! Success! But why is she so pale?"

He rose and drew aside the window curtain and suffered the light of natural day to fall into the room and rest upon Georgiana's cheek. Slowly she unclosed her eyes and gazed into the mirror that her husband now gave her. A faint smile flitted over her lips. But then her eyes sought Aylmer's face with a trouble and anxiety that he did not understand.

"My poor Aylmer," she murmured.

"Poor? No, I am the richest, happiest husband. Do you not see? It is a success. You are a perfect woman."

"My poor Aylmer," she repeated. "You have aimed high. Do not repent that. But you have rejected the best that earth could offer."

He knelt beside her on the couch and took her hand. Her fingers were cold. "Rejected you? Never!"

"I am dying."

Alas! It was too true. The fatal hand had grappled with the mystery of life.

The presence of the birthmark had been awful to him; its departure now was more awful still. Watch the stain of the rainbow fading out of the sky, and you will know how that mysterious symbol faded from Georgiana's face. As the last crimson tint of the birthmark faded from her cheek, the parting breath of the now perfect woman passed into the atmosphere, and her soul, lingering a moment near her husband, took its heavenward flight.

On the laboratory table, the geranium was bone dry. Its fallen leaves lay like autumn about its base of clay.

ARRESTED

by Ambrose Bierce

*A posse with a pack of bloodhounds was on
his track. His chance of escape was slender.*

Orrin Brower of Kentucky was a fugitive from justice.
A jury had found him guilty of murdering his
brother-in-law and had sentenced him to hang by the
neck until dead. But on the night before he was to die,
Brower made a daring escape. He knocked down his
jailer with an iron bar, robbed him of his keys, and, opening the outer door, walked out into the dark night.

Neither moon nor stars were visible. Brower ran for the
forest beyond town. But he was not from this part of the
state, and he was soon lost. He could not tell if he was
running away from the town or back toward it. He knew
that in either case, a posse of citizens with a pack of

bloodhounds would soon be on his track, and his chance of escape was very slender, for the jailer he had struck with the iron bar had been unarmed.

Brower had no weapon now with which to defend himself. Yet he thought that even an added hour of freedom was well worth having.

Just then, as he emerged from the thick wood onto an old road, he saw a man standing motionless in the gloom. It was too late for Brower to retreat. The fugitive felt that at the first movement back toward the wood he would be filled with buckshot. For a long moment, the two men stood as trees. Brower was nearly suffocated by the activity of his own pounding heart.

A moment later—though it seemed like an hour—the moon sailed into a patch of unclouded sky. The hunted saw that the other man was Burton Duff, the jailer that Brower had struck with the bar. The jailer was as white as death, and upon his brow was the livid mark where the iron bar had cracked open his skull.

The jailer raised an arm and pointed. Brower understood. He was a courageous criminal. That much was obvious from his escape. But even a criminal, when beaten, submits.

Turning his back to his captor, Brower walked submissively away in the direction indicated, looking neither to the right nor to the left, hardly daring to breathe. His head ached with the imagined pain of being shot in the back should he attempt again to flee from his jailer.

Eventually, they entered the town, which was all alight but deserted. Straight toward the jail the criminal walked. He laid his hand upon the knob of the heavy iron door of the main entrance, pushed it open, and entered.

A half-dozen men, armed, were in the room. They faced him, amazed. Brower turned to look over his shoulder at the man who had brought him back, but nobody was there. No one at all was behind him.

But there, on the floor in the corridor, exactly where Brower had left him, lay the dead body of Burton Duff.

THE RIGHT KIND
OF HOUSE

by Henry Slesar

Rotted beams, blistered paint, wet basement—
Sadie Grimes's house was a real fixer-upper.
Who would ever want to buy it?

The automobile that stopped in front of Aaron
Hacker's real estate office had New York license
plates. Aaron didn't need to see the license plates to know
that its owner was new to the elm-shaded town of Ivy
Corners. The car was a red convertible. There was nothing else like it in town.

The man got out of the car and headed straight for the
door.

"It seems to be a customer," said Mr. Hacker to the
young lady at the other desk. "Let's look busy."

It was a customer, all right. The man had a folded

newspaper in his right hand. He was a bit on the heavy side and wore a light gray suit. He was about fifty with dark, curly hair. The skin of his face was flushed and hot, but his narrow eyes were frosty-clear.

He opened the door and nodded at Aaron. "Are you Mr. Hacker?"

"Yes, sir," Aaron smiled. "What can I do for you?"

The man waved the newspaper. "I saw the name of your agency in the real estate section of the newspaper."

"Yep. I take an ad every week. Lots of city people are interested in a town like ours, Mr. —"

"Waterbury," the man said. He pulled a handkerchief from his pocket and mopped his face. "Hot today."

"Unusually hot," Aaron answered. "Doesn't often get so hot in our town. We're near the lake, you know. Well, won't you sit down, Mr. Waterbury?"

"Thank you." The man took the chair and sighed. "I've been driving around. Thought I'd look the town over before I came in. Very nice little place."

"Yes, we like it," said Aaron.

"Now I really don't have much time, Mr. Hacker. Suppose we get right down to business. I saw a house at the edge of town, across the way from an old deserted building."

"Was it an old yellow house with pillars?" asked Aaron.

"That's the place. Do you have that house listed?"

Aaron chuckled softly. "Yep, we got it listed." He flipped through a looseleaf book and pointed to a type-written sheet. "But you won't be interested for long."

"Why not?"

Aaron turned the book around. "Read it for yourself."

"Authentic colonial," the man read. "Eight rooms, two baths, large porches, trees and shrubbery. Near shopping and schools. $300,000."

"Still interested?"

The man stirred uncomfortably. "Why not? Something wrong with it?"

"Well." Aaron scratched his temple. "If you really like this town, Mr. Waterbury—I mean if you really want to settle here, I have any number of places that'd suit you better."

"Now, just a minute!" The man looked indignant. "I'm asking you about this colonial house. You want to sell it or not?"

"Do I?" Aaron chuckled. "Mister, I've had that property on my hands for five years. There's no house I'd rather collect a commission on. Only my luck ain't that good."

"What do you mean?"

"I mean you won't buy. That's what I mean. I keep the listing on my books just for the sake of old Sadie Grimes. Otherwise, I wouldn't waste the space. Believe me."

"I don't get you."

"Then let me explain. Mrs. Grimes put her place up for sale five years ago, when her son died. She gave me the job of selling it. I told her then that the old place ain't even worth *$50,000!*"

The man swallowed. "And she wants *$300,000?*"

"That's right. It's a real old house. I mean old. Some of the beams rotted. Basement's full of water half the time. Upper floor leans to the right about five inches. And the grounds are a mess. Not that it couldn't be fixed up, you understand. But the price has got to be right. And it isn't. I told her that right to her face."

"But why does she want so much?"

Aaron shrugged. "Sentiment, I suppose. The house has been in her family since the Revolution."

The man looked at the floor. "That's too bad," he said. He looked up at Aaron and smiled sheepishly. "And I kinda liked the place. It was—I don't know how to explain it—the right kind of house."

"I know what you mean. It's a friendly old place. A good buy at $50,000, but $300,000?" He laughed. "I think I know Sadie's reasoning, though. You see, she doesn't have much money. Her son was supporting her, doing well in the city. Then he died suddenly, and she knew it was sensible to sell. But she couldn't bring herself to part with the old place. So she set a price tag so high that nobody would buy it. That eased her conscience." Mr. Hacker shook his head softly. "It's a strange world, ain't it?"

"Yes," Waterbury said thoughtfully. Then he stood up. "Tell you what, Mr. Hacker. Suppose I drive out to see Mrs. Grimes? Suppose I talk to her about it, get her to change her price."

"You're fooling yourself, Mr. Waterbury. I've been trying for years."

"Who knows? Maybe if somebody else tried—"

Aaron Hacker shrugged his shoulders. "Who *knows,* is right. It's a strange world, Mr. Waterbury. If you're willing to go to the trouble, I'll be only too happy to lend a hand. Just let me ring Sadie. I'll tell her you're on your way."

☠

Waterbury parked his car beside the rotted picket fence that faced Sadie Grimes's house. The lawn was a jungle of weeds and crabgrass, and the columns that rose from the front porch were covered with flaking paint. He reached for the hand knocker on the door and banged it twice.

The woman who came to the door was short and plump. Her hair was white and her face was lined. She wore a heavy wool sweater, despite the heat. "You must be Mr. Waterbury," she said.

The man smiled. "How do you do, Mrs. Grimes?"

"About as well as I can expect. I suppose you want to come in?"

☠

"It's awfully hot out here." He chuckled.

"Hm. Well, come in then. I've put some lemonade in the icebox. Only don't expect me to bargain with you, Mr. Waterbury. I'm not that kind of person."

"Of course not," the man said, following her inside.

They entered a square parlor with heavy furniture. The only color in the room was in the faded hues of the worn rug in the center of the floor. The old woman headed straight for a rocker and sat motionless, her wrinkled hands folded sternly. "Well?" she said. "If you have anything to say, Mr. Waterbury, I suggest you say it."

The man cleared his throat. "Mrs. Grimes, I've just spoken with your real estate agent...."

"I know all that," she snapped. "Aaron's a fool. All the more for letting you come here with the notion of changing my mind. I'm too old for changing my mind, Mr. Waterbury."

"Er—well, I don't know if that was my intention, Mrs. Grimes. I thought we'd just—talk a little."

She leaned back, and the rocker squeaked. "Talk's free. Say what you like."

"Yes." He mopped his face again, and shoved the handkerchief back into his pocket. "Well, let me put it this way, Mrs. Grimes. I'm a businessman, a bachelor, never married; I live alone. I've worked for a long time, and I've made a fair amount of money. Now I'm ready to retire—

☠

to somewhere quiet. I like Ivy Corners. I passed through here some years ago on my way to—er, Albany. I thought one day I might like to settle here."

"So?"

"So, when I drove through your town today, and saw this house, it just seemed—right for me."

"I like it too, Mr. Waterbury. That's why I'm asking a fair price for it."

Waterbury blinked. "Fair price? You'll have to admit, Mrs. Grimes, these days a house like this shouldn't cost more than—"

"That's enough!" the woman cried. "I told you, Mr. Waterbury, I don't want to sit here all day and argue with you. If you won't pay my price, then we can forget all about it."

"But, Mrs. Grimes—"

"Good day, Mr. Waterbury!" She stood up, indicating that he was expected to leave.

But he didn't. "Wait a minute, Mrs. Grimes," he said. "Just a moment. I know it's crazy, but—all right. I'll pay what you want."

She looked at him for a long moment. "Are you sure, Mr. Waterbury?"

"Positive! I've enough money. If that's the only way you'll have it, that's the way it'll be."

She smiled. "I think that lemonade'll be cold enough.

I'll bring you some—and then I'll tell you something about this house."

He was mopping his brow when she returned with the tray. He gulped at the frosty yellow beverage greedily.

"This house," she said, easing back in her rocker, "has been in my family since 1802. It was built fifteen years before that. Every member of the family, except my son, Michael, was born in the bedroom upstairs. After Michael was born, there was a flood in the basement, and we never seemed to get it dry since. I love the old place, though, you understand."

"Of course," Waterbury said.

"Michael's father died when Michael was nine. There were hard times then. I did some needlework, and my own father had left me some money, which supports me today. Not in grand style, but I manage. Michael missed his father, perhaps even more than I. He grew up to be, well, wild is the only word that comes to mind."

The man nodded in understanding.

"When he graduated from high school, Michael left Ivy Corners and went to the city. He went there against my wishes, make no mistake. But he was like so many young men—full of ambition, wild ambition. I didn't know what he did in the city. But he must have been successful—he sent me money regularly. However, I didn't see him for nine years."

"Ah," the man sighed, sadly.

"Yes, it wasn't easy for me. But it was even worse when Michael came home. Because, when he did, he was in trouble."

"Oh?"

"I didn't know how bad the trouble was. He showed up in the middle of the night, looking thinner and older than I could have believed possible."

Waterbury took another gulp of lemonade, wondering how much longer he would have to listen to the old woman talk. He suddenly felt very tired.

"He had no luggage with him," she continued. "Only a small black suitcase. When I tried to take it from him, he almost struck me. Struck me—his own mother!" She leaned forward in the rocker to stare into Waterbury's sweating face. "I put him to bed myself, as if he were a little boy again. I could hear him crying out during the night. The next day, he told me to leave the house. Just for a few hours. He wanted to do something, he said. He didn't explain what. But when I returned that evening, I noticed that the black suitcase was gone."

The man's eyes widened over the lemonade glass. "What did it mean?" he asked.

"I didn't know then. But I found out soon, too terribly soon. That night, a man came to our house. I don't even know how he got in. I first knew when I heard voices in Michael's room. I went to the door, and tried to listen, tried to find out what sort of trouble my boy was in. But I heard only shouts and threats, and then..."

She paused, and her shoulders sagged.

"A shot," she continued, "a gunshot. When I went into the room, I found the bedroom window open and the stranger gone. And Michael—he was on the floor. He was dead!"

"Dead?" Waterbury croaked. His dry throat seemed to be tightening.

"That was five years ago," she said. "Five long years. It was a while before I realized what had happened. The police told me the story. Michael and this other man had been involved in a crime, a serious crime. They had stolen close to one million dollars."

Waterbury's chair creaked as he shifted uncomfortably. He was having trouble keeping his eyes open in this dreadful heat.

"Michael had taken that money, and run off with it. He wanted to keep it all for himself. He hid it somewhere in this house—to this very day I don't know where. The other man had come looking for my son, looking to collect his share. When he found the money gone, he—he killed my boy."

She sat back in her rocker. "That's when I put this house up for sale—at $300,000. I knew that, someday, my son's killer would return to look for the money. Someday, he would want this house at any price. All I had to do was wait until I found the man willing to pay much too much for an old lady's house."

She rocked gently.

Waterbury put down the empty glass and licked his lips. He was growing dizzy, very dizzy.

Sadie Grimes smiled sweetly. "More lemonade, Mr. Waterbury?"

"Oh!" he gasped, his throat closing on itself. "This lemonade … is so bitter."

BATTLEGROUND

by Stephen King

By Mr. King's request, "Battleground" appears in its entirety here and is not the abridged version that appeared in Read *magazine.*

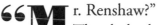r. Renshaw?"
The desk clerk's voice caught him halfway to the elevator, and Renshaw turned back impatiently, shifting his flight bag from one hand to the other. The envelope in his coat pocket, stuffed with twenties and fifties, crackled heavily. The job had gone well and the pay had been excellent—even after the Organization's 15 percent finder's fee had been skimmed off the top. Now all he wanted was a hot shower and a gin and tonic and sleep.

"What is it?"

"Package, sir. Would you sign the slip?"

Renshaw signed and looked thoughtfully at the rectangular package. His name and the building's address were written on the gummed label in a spiky backhand script that seemed familiar. He rocked the package on the imitation-marble surface of the desk, and something clanked faintly inside.

"Should I have that sent up, Mr. Renshaw?"

"No, I've got it." It was about eighteen inches on a side and fitted clumsily under his arm. He put it on the plush carpet that covered the elevator floor and twisted his key in the penthouse slot above the regular rack of buttons. The car rose smoothly and silently. He closed his eyes and let the job replay itself on the dark screen of his mind.

First, as always, a call from Cal Bates: "You available, Johnny?"

He was available twice a year, minimum fee $10,000. He was very good, very reliable, but what his customers really paid for was the infallible predator's talent. John Renshaw was a human hawk, constructed by both genetics and environment to do two things superbly: kill and survive.

After Bates's call, a buff-colored envelope appeared in Renshaw's box. A name, an address, a photograph. All committed to memory; then down the garbage disposal with the ashes of envelope and contents.

This time the face had been that of a sallow Miami businessman named Hans Morris, founder and owner of the Morris Toy Company. Someone had wanted Morris out of the way and had gone to the Organization. The Organization, in the person of Calvin Bates, had talked to John Renshaw. *Pow.* Mourners please omit flowers.

The door slid open, he picked up his package and stepped out. He unlocked the suite and stepped in. At this time of day, just after 3 P.M., the spacious living room was splashed with April sunshine. He paused for a moment, enjoying it, then put the package on the end table by the door and loosened his tie. He dropped the envelope on top of it and walked over to the terrace.

He pushed open the sliding glass door and stepped out. It was cold, and the wind knifed through his thin topcoat. Yet he paused a moment, looking over the city the way a general might survey a captured country. Traffic crawled beetlelike in the streets. Far away, almost buried in the golden afternoon haze, the Bay Bridge glittered like a madman's mirage. To the east, all but lost behind the downtown high rises, the crammed and dirty tenements with their stainless-steel forests of TV aerials. It was better up here. Better than in the gutters.

He went back inside, slid the door closed, and went into the bathroom for a long, hot shower.

When he sat down forty minutes later to regard his package, drink in hand, the shadows had marched halfway across the wine-colored carpet and the best of the afternoon was past.

It was a bomb.

Of course it wasn't, but one proceeded as if it were. That was why one had remained healthy and upright and taking nourishment while so many others had gone to that great unemployment office in the sky.

If it was a bomb, it was clockless. It sat utterly silent; bland and enigmatic. Plastique was more likely these days, anyway. Less temperamental than the clocksprings manufactured by Westclox and Big Ben.

Renshaw looked at the postmark. Miami, April 15. Five days ago. So the bomb was not time-set. It would have gone off in the hotel safe in that case.

Miami. Yes. And that spiky backhand writing. There had been a framed photograph on the sallow businessman's desk. The photo had been of an even sallower old crone wearing a babushka. The script slanted across the bottom had read: "Best from your number-one idea girl—Mom."

What kind of number-one idea is this, Mom? A do-it-yourself extermination kit?

He regarded the package with complete concentration, not moving, his hands folded. Extraneous questions, such as how Morris' number-one idea girl might have discovered his address, did not occur to him. They were for later, for Cal Bates. Unimportant now.

With a sudden, almost absent move, he took a small

celluloid calendar out of his wallet and inserted it deftly under the twine that crisscrossed the brown paper. He slid it under the Scotch tape that held one end flap. The flap came loose, relaxing against the twine.

He paused for a time, observing, then leaned close and sniffed. Cardboard, paper, string. Nothing more. He walked around the box, squatted easily on his haunches, and repeated the process. Twilight was invading his apartment with gray, shadowy fingers.

One of the flaps popped free of the restraining twine, showing a dull green box beneath. Metal. Hinged. He produced a pocket knife and cut the twine. It fell away, and a few helping prods with the tip of the knife revealed the box.

It was green with black markings, and stenciled on the front in white letters were the words: G.I. JOE VIETNAM FOOTLOCKER. Below that: 20 Infantrymen, 10 Helicopters, 2 BAR Men, 2 Bazooka Men, 2 Medics, 4 Jeeps. Below that: a flag decal. Below that, in the corner: Morris Toy Company, Miami, Fla.

He reached out to touch it, then withdrew his hand. Something inside the footlocker had moved.

Renshaw stood up, not hurrying, and backed across the room toward the kitchen and the hall. He snapped on the lights.

The Vietnam Footlocker was rocking, making the

brown paper beneath it rattle. It suddenly overbalanced and fell to the carpet with a soft thud, landing on one end. The hinged top opened a crack of perhaps two inches.

Tiny foot soldiers, about an inch and a half tall, began to crawl out. Renshaw watched them, unblinking. His mind made no effort to cope with the real or unreal aspect of what he was seeing—only with the possible consequences for his survival.

The soldiers were wearing minuscule army fatigues, helmets, and field packs. Tiny carbines were slung across their shoulders. Two of them looked briefly across the room at Renshaw. Their eyes, no bigger than pencil points, glittered.

Five, ten, twelve, then all twenty. One of them was gesturing, ordering the others. They lined themselves up along the crack that the fall had produced and began to push. The crack began to widen.

Renshaw picked one of the large pillows off the couch and began to walk toward them. The commanding officer turned and gestured. The others whirled and unslung their carbines. There were tiny, almost delicate popping sounds, and Renshaw felt suddenly as if he had been stung by bees.

He threw the pillow. It struck them, knocking them sprawling, then hit the box, and knocked it wide open. Insectlike, with a faint, high whirring noise like chiggers, a cloud of miniature helicopters, painted jungle green, rose out of the box.

Tiny *phut! phut!* sounds reached Renshaw's ears and he saw pinprick-sized muzzle flashes coming from the open copter doors. Needles pricked his belly, his right arm, the side of his neck. He clawed out and got one—sudden pain in his fingers; blood welling. The whirling blades had chopped them to the bone in diagonal scarlet hash marks. The others whirled out of range, circling him like horse-flies. The stricken copter thumped to the rug and lay still.

Sudden excruciating pain in his foot made him cry out. One of the foot soldiers was standing on his shoe and bay-oneting his ankle. The tiny face looked up, panting and grinning.

Renshaw kicked at it and the tiny body flew across the room to splatter on the wall. It did not leave blood but a viscid purple smear.

There was a tiny, coughing explosion and blinding agony ripped his thigh. One of the bazooka men had come out of the footlocker. A small curl of smoke rose lazily from his weapon. Renshaw looked down at his leg and saw a blackened, smoking hole in his pants the size of a quarter. The flesh beneath was charred.

The little bastard shot me!

He turned and ran into the hall, then into his bed-room. One of the helicopters buzzed past his cheek, blades whirring busily. The small stutter of a BAR. Then it darted away.

The gun beneath his pillow was a .44 Magnum, big enough to put a hole the size of two fists through anything it hit. Renshaw turned, holding the pistol in his hands. He realized coolly that he would be shooting at a moving target not much bigger than a flying light bulb.

Two of the copters whirred in. Sitting on the bed, Renshaw fired once. One of the helicopters exploded into nothingness. That's two, he thought. He drew a bead on the second... squeezed the trigger...

It jigged! God, it jigged!

The helicopter swooped at him in a sudden deadly arc, fore and aft overhead props whirring with blinding speed. Renshaw caught a glimpse of one of the BAR men crouched at the open bay door, firing his weapon in short, deadly bursts, and then he threw himself to the floor and rolled.

My eyes, the bastard was going for my eyes!

He came up on his back at the far wall, the gun held at chest level. But the copter was retreating. It seemed to pause for a moment, and dip in recognition of Renshaw's superior firepower. Then it was gone, back toward the living room.

Renshaw got up, wincing as his weight came down on the wounded leg. It was bleeding freely. And why not? he thought grimly. It's not everybody who gets hit point-blank with a bazooka shell and lives to tell about it.

So Mom was his number-one idea girl, was she? She was all that and a bit more.

He shook a pillowcase free of the tick and ripped it into a bandage for his leg, then took his shaving mirror from the bureau and went to the hallway door. Kneeling, he shoved it out onto the carpet at an angle and peered in.

They were bivouacking by the footlocker, damned if they weren't. Miniature soldiers ran hither and thither, setting up tents. Jeeps two inches high raced about importantly. A medic was working over the soldier Renshaw had kicked. The remaining eight copters flew in a protective swarm overhead, at coffee-table level.

Suddenly they became aware of the mirror, and three of the foot soldiers dropped to one knee and began firing. Seconds later the mirror shattered in four places. *Okay, okay, then.*

Renshaw went back to the bureau and got the heavy mahogany odds-and-ends box Linda had given him for Christmas. He hefted it once, nodded, and went to the doorway and lunged through. He wound up and fired like a pitcher throwing a fast ball. The box described a swift, true vector and smashed little men like ninepins. One of the jeeps rolled over twice. Renshaw advanced to the doorway of the living room, sighted on one of the sprawling soldiers, and gave it to him.

Several of the others had recovered. Some were kneeling and firing formally. Others had taken cover. Still others had retreated back into the footlocker.

The bee stings began to pepper his legs and torso, but none reached higher than his rib cage. Perhaps the range was too great. It didn't matter; he had no intention of being turned away. This was it.

He missed with his next shot—they were so small—but the following one sent another soldier into a broken sprawl.

The copters were buzzing toward him ferociously. Now the tiny bullets began to splat into his face, above and below his eyes. He potted the lead copter, then the second. Jagged streaks of pain silvered his vision.

The remaining six split into two retreating wings. His face was wet with blood and he swiped at it with his forearm. He was ready to start firing again when he paused. The soldiers who had retreated inside the footlocker were trundling something out. Something that looked like…

There was a blinding sizzle of yellow fire, and a sudden gust of wood and plaster exploded from the wall to his left.

… *a rocket launcher!*

He squeezed off one shot at it, missed, wheeled and ran for the bathroom at the far end of the corridor. He slammed the door and locked it. In the bathroom-mirror an Indian was staring back at him with dazed and haunted eyes, a battle crazed Indian with thin streamers of red paint drawn from holes no bigger than grains of pepper. A ragged flap of skin dangled from one cheek. There was a gouged furrow in his neck.

I'm losing!

He ran a shaking hand through his hair. The front door was cut off. So was the phone and the kitchen extension. They had a rocket launcher and a direct hit would tear his head off.

Damn it, that wasn't even listed on the box!

He started to draw in a long breath and let it out in a sudden grunt as a fist-sized section of the door blew in with a charred burst of wood. Tiny flames glowed briefly around the ragged edges of the hole, and he saw the brilliant flash as they launched another round. More wood blew inward, scattering burning slivers on the bathroom rug. He stamped them out and two of the copters buzzed angrily through the hole. Minuscule BAR slugs stitched his chest.

With a whining groan of rage he smashed one out of the air barehanded, sustaining a picket fence of deep slashes across his palm. In sudden desperate invention, he slung a heavy bath towel over the other. It fell, writhing, to the floor, and he stamped the life out of it. His breath was coming in hoarse whoops. Blood ran into one eye, hot and stinging, and he wiped it away.

There. There. That'll make them think.

Indeed, it did seem to be making them think. There was no movement for fifteen minutes. Renshaw sat on the edge of the tub, thinking feverishly. There had to be a way out of this blind alley. There *had* to be. If there was only a way to flank them...

He suddenly turned and looked at the small window over the tub. There was a way. Of course there was.

His eyes dropped to the can of lighter fluid on top of the medicine cabinet. He was reaching for it when the rustling noise came.

He whirled, bringing the Magnum up...but it was only a tiny scrap of paper shoved under the crack of the door. The crack, Renshaw noted grimly, was too narrow for even one of *them* to get through.

There was one tiny word written on the paper:

Surrender

Renshaw smiled grimly and put the lighter fluid in his breast pocket. There was a chewed stub of pencil beside it. He scrawled one word on the paper and shoved it back under the door. The word was:

NUTS

There was a suddenly blinding barrage of rocket shells, and Renshaw backed away. They arched through the hole in the door and detonated against the pale blue tiles above the towel rack, turning the elegant wall into a pocket lunar landscape. Renshaw threw a hand over his eyes as plaster flew in a hot rain of shrapnel. Burning holes ripped through his shirt and his back was peppered.

When the barrage stopped, Renshaw moved. He climbed on top of the tub and slid the window open. Cold stars looked in at him. It was a narrow window, and a narrow ledge beyond it. But there was no time to think of that.

He boosted himself through, and the cold air slapped his lacerated face and neck like an open hand. He was leaning over the balance point of his hands, staring straight down. Forty stories down. From this height the street looked no wider than a child's train track. The bright, winking lights of the city glittered madly below him like thrown jewels.

With the deceptive ease of a trained gymnast, Renshaw brought his knees up to rest on the lower edge of the window. If one of those wasp-sized copters flew through that hole in the door now, one shot in the ass would send him straight down, screaming all the way.

None did.

He twisted, thrust one leg out, and one reaching hand grabbed the overhead cornice and held. A moment later he was standing on the ledge outside the window.

Deliberately not thinking of the horrifying drop below his heels, not thinking of what would happen if one of the helicopters buzzed out after him, Renshaw edged toward the corner of the building.

Fifteen feet...ten...There. He paused, his chest pressed against the wall, hands splayed out on the rough surface. He could feel the lighter fluid in his breast pocket and the reassuring weight of the Magnum jammed in his waistband.

Now to get around the corner.

Gently, he eased one foot around and slid his weight onto it. Now the right angle was pressed razorlike into his chest and gut. There was a smear of bird guano in front of his eyes on the rough stone. Christ, he thought crazily. I didn't know they could fly this high.

His left foot slipped.

For a weird, timeless moment, he tottered over the brink, right arm backwatering madly for balance, and then he was clutching the two sides of the building in a lover's embrace, face pressed against the hard corner, breath shuddering in and out of his lungs.

A bit at a time, he slid the other foot around.

Thirty feet away, his own living-room terrace jutted out.

He made his way down to it, breath sliding in and out of his lungs with shallow force. Twice he was forced to stop as sharp gusts of wind tried to pick him off the ledge.

Then he was there, gripping the ornamented iron railings.

He hoisted himself over noiselessly. He had left the curtains half drawn across the sliding glass partition, and now he peered in cautiously. They were just the way he wanted them—ass to.

Four soldiers and one copter had been left to guard the footlocker. The rest would be outside the bathroom door with the rocket launcher.

Okay. In through the opening like gangbusters. Wipe out the ones by the footlocker, then out the door. Then a quick taxi to the airport. Off to Miami to find Morris' number-one idea girl. He thought he might just burn her face off with a flame thrower. That would be poetic justice.

He took off his shirt and ripped a long strip from one sleeve. He dropped the rest to flutter limply by his feet, and bit off the plastic spout on the can of lighter fluid. He stuffed one end of the rag inside, withdrew it, and stuffed the other end in so only a six-inch strip of saturated cotton hung free.

He got out his lighter, took a deep breath, and thumbed the wheel. He tipped it to the cloth and as it sprang alight he rammed open the glass partition and plunged through.

The copter reacted instantly, kamikaze-diving him as he charged across the rug, dripping tiny splatters of liquid fire. Renshaw straight-armed it, hardly noticing the jolt of pain that ran up his arm as the turning blades chopped his flesh open.

The tiny foot soldiers scattered into the footlocker.

After that, it all happened very rapidly.

Renshaw threw the lighter fluid. The can caught, mushrooming into a licking fireball. The next instant he was reversing, running for the door.

He never knew what hit him.

It was like the thud that a steel safe would make when dropped from a respectable height. Only this thud ran through the entire high-rise apartment building, thrumming in its steel frame like a tuning fork.

The penthouse door blew off its hinges and shattered against the far wall.

A couple who had been walking hand in hand below looked up in time to see a very large white flash, as though a hundred flashing guns had gone off at once.

"Somebody blew a fuse," the man said. "I guess—"

"What's that?" his girl asked.

Something was fluttering lazily down toward them; he caught it in one outstretched hand. "Jesus, some guy's shirt. All full of little holes. Bloody, too."

"I don't like it," she said nervously. "Call a cab, huh, Ralph? We'll have to talk to the cops if something happened up there, and I ain't supposed to be out with you."

"Sure, yeah."

He looked around, saw a taxi, and whistled. Its brake lights flared and they ran across to get it.

Behind them, unseen, a tiny scrap of paper floated down and landed near the remains of John Renshaw's shirt. Spiky backhand script read:

Hey, kids! Special in this Vietnam Footlocker!
(For a Limited Time Only)
1 Rocket Launcher
20 Surface-to-air-"Twister" Missiles
1 Scale-Model Thermonuclear Weapon

PART III
ATROPOS,
TRIMMER OF THREADS

THE BARGAIN

A retelling of the Greek myth of
Admetus and the Shadow of Death

He had until dawn to find someone to take his place.
Surely there must be one person who loved him
enough to agree to the bargain.

Admetus was young, not old. He was healthy, not ill. Solid muscles shaped his arms, back, chest, and legs. He had just assumed power as King of Pherae in ancient Greece. And he had just married the most beautiful woman. Together they would have sons who would be heroes. Yes, Admetus had many sweet reasons to live.

But during the night, the shadow of Death came for Admetus. "Your hour has struck, Admetus," the tall shadow whispered in his ear. "You must die."

Admetus woke in a cold sweat, thinking surely the

voice he had heard came from a nightmare. But the shadow still hovered over him. "Come," he beckoned. "Come now."

"No!" Admetus cried. "I am not ready! Take another whose life is less valuable than mine!"

The shadow disliked such arrogance in mortals. Nevertheless, he was willing to bargain. "If you can find one person to take your place, I will spare your life. You have until dawn."

Then the shadow dissolved.

Admetus looked at his wife asleep beside him. Life without her would not be life at all. But there were others in the palace who also adored him. He was their king. Surely they would die for him.

Admetus hurried down the cold marble floors to the room where the old nurse who had cared for him during his childhood coughed in her sleep. The woman's lips were cracked, and her eyes were yellow with sickness. Admetus woke her. "The shadow of Death has come for me. But if you take my place, I will live."

The nurse sobbed when she heard that Admetus must die. "You are so young, so strong."

"And you are so old, so ill. Dying will be a peaceful sleep for you."

"Each breath I take may be my last," the old nurse admitted. "But that is why each breath is a gift I cherish."

"You will not do it? You will not take my place?"

The old nurse hacked and wheezed. "No, life is precious, even to my old bones."

Outside the window Admetus heard the first cries of the birds. It was almost dawn. He hurried next to his parents' chambers. "You gave me life once," he pleaded with them. "You can give me life again."

"You think that because we are old we no longer enjoy the warm sun on our faces? Oh, Admetus, our son, we will miss you terribly, terribly," his parents cried.

The pink streaks of dawn were just now creeping over the horizon. Admetus returned to his bed. His wife reached for him. "Let me hold you one last time," she cried. "My sweet husband."

She slipped her arms around him. Her hands felt so cold.

"How did you know?" he asked.

"I heard the shadow come for you during the night," she answered in a voice that was thin and weak.

"I asked the old nurse. I asked my parents. No one would give me my life back."

"Why didn't you ask me, Admetus?"

"You?" He looked at his beautiful wife, the woman who would give him sons that would be heroes. In the growing light of morning, her face was ghostly pale. "No, not you."

"Did you not think I loved you enough to take your place?" she asked.

Admetus saw then the poison hemlock and the empty cup from which she had drunk. "No!" he cried, hugging her to him, but she was already cold in his arms.

The tall shadow had returned. "So, you have found someone who valued your life over her own," the shadow spoke. "You will live, Admetus." The shadow raised his arms and covered Admetus's dead wife, still cradled in his arms.

"You can't have her!" the king shouted. "Get back. She is mine."

"You agreed to the bargain," the shadow said.

The first rays of sunlight seeped through the curtained window. "No!" Admetus cried. "I take it back. Life without her is no life at all!"

But the shadow and the only woman Admetus would ever love were gone.

REVERSE INSOMNIA

by Jonathon Blake

All he could do was sleep, and sleep some more.
It didn't make any sense, especially the dreams.

Here I am again.

I've slept for two days straight this time. I'm beginning to believe that this may be unhealthy. The doctor says I have "reverse insomnia," but he also looks at me as if I were crazy.

I don't trust my doctor. *He* looks crazy. We just sit in his office and eyeball each other, wondering how crazy we both really are. Until he gives me some pills and tells me it's reverse insomnia.

I hate that idiot doctor.

His pills don't help. Did I mention that I slept for two days straight? Right through my son Andy's birthday. Right through the cake and ice cream and presents and everything.

Julie was upset with me. But I just shrugged and apologized. What could I do? I was asleep. I really think something's wrong. It's happening more and more frequently every week. A day of sleep here, two days there. It's crazy.

Thank goodness I had a lot of off-time coming to me at the office. My boss is angry with me, though. Ever since I started having this abundance of sleep, my work has slipped. Well, truthfully, it's backslid terribly.

I'm a journalist, but for some reason the words aren't coming the way they used to. The other day I thought I'd written a fantastic article on drunken driving and violence in the United States. Turns out all I'd written was a single word in the middle of a snow-white sheet.

Crash.

I couldn't make any sense of it. Neither could my boss.

I've got to get up and eat. I want Bran Flakes, but I can't recall which cabinet they're in. Everything is a little fuzzy at the edges.

There's Julie sitting on the couch in the den. Geez, I love her. That's funny. She's dressed in black. Hmm, I thought she hated that color. In the pantry. Next to the refrigerator. That's where the Bran Flakes are. How strange. I was just about to ask Julie where the cereal was, but it just popped into my head. Go figure.

Andy's sitting at the kitchen table eating Fruit Loops and chocolate kisses. I want to tell him to stop, but I'm ashamed, having missed his birthday and all.

Andy has a black balloon wrapped around his tiny right wrist. For some reason, I feel like crying.

Later, the helium must have found a way out somehow. The balloon floats, almost touching the table, looking like a shrunken head, wrinkled and distorted.

I don't want cereal anymore. In fact, I'm sure the Bran Flakes taste like cardboard now. I hate them. But not as much as I hate that doctor.

I look at Andy again. Now his forehead is touching the table. His left hand is gently resting in his bowl of Fruit Loops. Droplets of milk are clinging to his skin, making his hand and arm seem surrealistically white.

I want to reach out and draw Andy up in my arms, but I can't. I know I shouldn't touch him, but I don't know why. He seems very distant, far away. The balloon is no longer attached to his wrist. Instead, he wears a watch. I get close enough to look over his shoulder. 12:42. It says 12:42. His watch has stopped. I must remember to send his watch to the store to be fixed.

Suddenly, now I am standing beside Julie. She's still on the couch, watching television. The screen is blank, black, yet she stares at it as if it were the most important thing in the world. I want to speak to her, ask her how her day was, but I know I shouldn't. Or maybe I can't. Instead, I look at the black screen too.

Julie says she's fine, but her lips never move. I tell her I'm fine too, but the words never reach my mouth.

Julie nods her head, and suddenly the television lights up. I see a small child standing in a field of white grass. He is dressed entirely in black. So is Julie; she's there too. The boy is holding a large black balloon with green numbers printed on it.

I strain to see the boy and the numbers.

It's Andy. The balloon reads 12:42.

I blink, and Julie is gone. The TV shuts off. Andy is gone. The kitchen is empty. Have I fallen asleep again? I just don't know.

I have to find out what time it is! But my watch, like Andy's, is broken. The numbers stare at me as if I am somehow wrong, deathly wrong.

"12:42. *12:42!*"

I can't breathe! I am surrounded by clocks. Clocks upon clocks upon clocks. "12:42," they are singing to me. "12:42!" they scream. And I begin to scream along with them.

Suddenly, I am in my bed. I must have been sleeping. Or dreaming.

I climb out of bed and see that I am wearing black silk pajamas. I don't recall ever changing into these. Then again, I don't remember anything but black.

I slowly walk to Andy's room. The door is shut. I hear crying.

I knock, but no one answers my call. I knock louder. Still, no answer. I open the door. The room is bare, white. All of it—the floor, the ceiling, the walls. White.

☠

I am in bed again, naked. My left leg itches uncomfortably and is very, very cold. Julie is lying next to me. Her lips are blue, like fingers of clay.

I swing my legs over the side of the bed and grab a robe that once was red. It has faded to gray, dark gray. If I didn't know any better, I'd say it was black.

I am staring at the doctor in his linoleum room. He tells me I am crazy and gives me some pills. He says I have reverse insomnia again. I throw the pills away, but they never hit the ground. Instead, the doctor opens his mouth and swallows them whole. His mouth becomes wider and wider until the whole room is sucked into his orifice.

The doctor swallows me.

I'm back in Andy's room, but this time it looks as it should—a bunk bed, a dresser, model airplanes I helped him make hanging from the ceiling. Andy is sitting on his bed coloring. I quietly step over the little cars on his floor, noticing that he had been playing demolition derby again. I look at the page he is so busily scribbling on. In large dark letters is the word *CRASH.*

I have to eat something. I go back to the kitchen. On

☠

the expansive kitchen table are three white cots. I don't remember Julie buying new furniture. And why would she have put cots on the kitchen table? Are they some kind of strange decorations?

The cots are disturbing somehow. They remind me of the crazy doctor and his stupid pills. The brightness of the white cots becomes all-consuming. My head begins to throb in time to the pulsing itch of my left leg.

I deny the existence of the furniture, try to block the cots out completely. It is better that way. But they loom before me with something new attached to each of them—large white intercoms. They remind me of my trip to Radio Shack with Julie and Andy. We were looking for a toy robot for Andy's birthday. The salesman was trying to sell me an intercom system for my home. He was very bothersome, and now all I can see are bright, bright lights.

I feel like a deer. Trapped. Transfixed by headlights, unable to run.

The intercoms are looking at me, accusing me. They stand there like all-powerful gods on their metal poles attached to the cots. A black sound oozes from them. I want to stop their noise. I have to stop them! But I cannot.

I listen.

"The woman and the boy were DOA, doctor. The

man is identified as Richard Young. He is comatose and has multiple contusions on the head and upper torso. His left leg was amputated. We had to do it. There was nothing we could do to save it. His condition is critical, sir."

The doctor's voice comes through another intercom. "How did it happen?"

From the third intercom: "Drunken driver. Hit the family head-on coming out of a shopping mall parking lot.

"Estimated time of death for the woman and boy—12:42."

The oozing black noise ceases.

A plug dangles like a limp snake from one of the white cots. It is plugged into everything and nothing.

Crying, I yank it forcefully.

Suddenly, I am asleep. Deep, deep asleep.

DEADLINE

by Richard Matheson

*The old man's story was fantastic, the confused
memory of a dying man. It could not possibly be true.*

There are two nights a year that a doctor just doesn't make plans—Christmas Eve and New Year's Eve. On Christmas Eve, the emergency was Bobby Dascouli's arm burns. I was cleaning and swathing them instead of nestling on the couch with Ruth, eyeing the twinkling colors of our Christmas tree. On New Year's Eve, the call from my answering service came ten minutes after I had arrived at a party at my sister's house. Ruth smiled sadly and shook her head. Then she kissed me on the cheek. "Poor Bill," she said.

"Poor Bill indeed," I grumbled and set down my glass of punch. I gently touched her much evident stomach.

"Don't go having our baby until I get back," I instructed. This was our first child, and although Ruth still had a few weeks yet before her due date, babies sometimes didn't pay attention to the calendar.

"I'll do my best to wait until after the New Year," she answered. "Be careful," she added. "The roads are snowy, and with so many people celebrating tonight.... "

"Don't worry about me. Just take care of yourself."

With wry acceptance, I said my hurried good-byes to everyone and left. I turned up the collar of my overcoat against the cold and crunched over the snowpacked side-walk to the car.

☠

It was after 11:00 when I reached a deserted East Main Street on the far side of town. I drove three blocks north to the address the service had given me and parked in front of what had once been an elegant apartment build-ing when my father was in practice. Now it was a ramshackle boardinghouse. Time had rusted through the gutters and rotted out the windowsills. Inside the lobby, the plaster was cracked and falling. The place smelled of must and decay.

I rang the landlady's bell and waited. A heavy woman appeared at the door. She wore a black sweater over her wrinkled green dress, striped anklets over her heavy sup-

☠

port stockings, saddle shoes over the anklets. She wore no makeup. The only color in her face was a chapped redness in her cheeks. Wisps of steel-gray hair hung across her temples.

She was a former patient of my father's, which is why she had asked for me. But we had never met. "You the doctor?" she asked.

I said I was.

"I'm the one who called. There's an old guy up on the fourth floor. He says he's dying."

"What room?" I asked, eager to make my visit and return to the more pleasant atmosphere of my sister Mary's house. To be honest, I was worried about Ruth. For two days, she had felt tired and achy. We had even considered not going to the New Year's Eve party at all.

"This way," the landlady said.

I followed her wheezing ascent up the stairs. We stopped in front of room 4-7, and she rapped on the thin paneling of the door, then pushed it open.

The old man was lying on an iron bed pushed against the wall. Even lying down, his body had the floppiness of a discarded doll. At his sides, frail hands lay motionless. His skin was the brown of old page edges, his face a wasted mask. On the bare pillow, his head lay still. His pale blue eyes were open, fixed on the cracked ceiling above him.

As I slipped off my coat, I saw that he was in no obvious pain. His expression was peaceful, accepting. I sat down on the bed and took his wrist. His eyes shifted as if just realizing I had come. He looked at me.

"Hello," I said and smiled.

"Hello."

The clearness of his voice startled me. However, his pulse was what I expected—a bare trickle of life, its beat barely felt beneath my pressing fingers. I set his hand back on the bed and leaned forward to place my palm against his forehead and to gaze into his eyes. He had no fever. He was not sick. He was only running down.

I patted the old man's shoulder reassuringly, then stood and gestured to the landlady. She clumped across the floor to the window.

"How long has he been in bed?" I asked her.

"Just since this afternoon," she answered. "That's what troubles me. It only began to happen this afternoon."

"What happened exactly?"

"He came down to my room and said he was going to die tonight."

I'd read about such a thing, how an old man or a woman announces that, at a certain time, they will die. And when that time comes, they do. Who knows what it is—a longing for death? A premonition? Perhaps a little of both.

"Has he any relatives?" I asked.

"None I know of," she said.

I nodded. It was not unusual for old folks to die alone. Suddenly, I was glad I had answered the call and had come.

"I don't get it," the landlady whispered.

"He is an old man. Everyone dies, eventually," I answered.

"No," she said. "When he first moved in about a month ago, he didn't look like he looks now, all wrinkled and gray. Even this afternoon he didn't look sick."

"He isn't in any pain. There really isn't anything I can do for him. It's just a matter of time."

"I see," she said.

I glanced at my watch—11:48. I thought of Ruth and that I should leave, but I hesitated. I glanced across the room at the figure in the bed. "How old is he anyway?" I asked. "Ninety? A hundred?"

"He never told me. And I never asked. I figure that's none of my business," she answered.

"I heard you," the old man said.

Both the woman and I turned, surprised.

"You want to know how old I am," the old man said. He opened his mouth to say something more, but a dry cough choked him.

A glass of water was on the bedside table, and I hurried to the old man's side, propped him up, and held the glass to his lips. When he had finished drinking, I gently laid his head back on the pillow.

"I'm one year old," he said.

I stared at his calm face. Then, I set the glass down on the table.

"You don't believe me," he said. "But it's true. I was born on December 31, 1996."

"You were?" I replied, thinking he was confused and really meant 1886.

"New Year's Eve, 1996," he repeated. Then he added, "At the stroke of midnight."

I felt a nervous shiver across my shoulders, as if for a split second my mind actually believed him.

The old man closed his eyes. "I've told a hundred people, and not one believes me. Not one understood."

I sat down on the edge of the bed once again. "Why not tell me about it," I offered. No one should die alone. As a doctor, the least I could do was provide the old man some comfort and company.

He drew in a breath slowly.

"A week after I was born, I was walking and talking. I was eating by myself. My mother and father couldn't believe their eyes."

"Well, that would be very advanced for a one-week-old," I said, humoring him.

"They took me to a doctor. I don't know what he

thought, but he didn't do anything. What could he do? I wasn't sick. I've never been sick. He sent me home with my mother and father."

"You remember this? Or is it something your parents told you long ago?" I asked.

The old man stared at the ceiling. "They were afraid of me."

"Who?"

"My mother and father."

I narrowed my eyes, studying the old man's face more closely, wondering where his story might lead. "Why were they afraid of you?"

"Because I grew old so quickly, too quickly. The doctors didn't know what to do. They called in specialists, but they didn't know what to do with me, either. I was a normal four-year-old boy, except I wasn't four years old. I was only weeks old."

The calmness and confidence of his voice suggested that the old man believed what he was saying. I felt another involuntary shiver through my body.

"They took tests. Made observations. I didn't see my parents anymore."

"You mean," I asked, trying to phrase the question gently, "your parents institutionalized you? Put you in a hospital?"

"Yes. Because, you see, I kept growing, aging. One

week I was six years old. The next week, I was eight. And then I was ten and twelve and fourteen."

The old man was delusional. His mind, like his body, had worn out, worn down. I thought it best not to encourage him to speak anymore. But he had begun his story and was determined now to finish it.

"After a while I figured it out," he said. "I understood what the doctors didn't. That's when I left the hospital. I walked out, because I knew there was nothing they could do to help me."

"What did you figure out?" I asked.

"That there have been men like me through all time. That's how the story got started," he said.

"What story?"

"About the old year and the new year. The old year is an old man with a beard and a scythe. And the new year is a little baby." The old man smiled weakly, as if remembering.

I heard a tire-screeching car in the street below, and I remembered how late it was—11:56—and Ruth's warning to be cautious about reckless drivers.

"People think it is a fable, but it isn't," the old man said. "There really are men who live for just one year. I don't know how it happens or why, but it does."

"What is your name?" I asked. It was foolish of me not to have asked it sooner.

"My name is unimportant. Who I am, what I am is." He

turned his worn face toward the wall. "I'm 1997," he said.

The landlady covered her mouth with her hand. I had quite forgotten that she was still in the room. Abruptly, as if caught in guilt, she turned and hurried out of the room. I watched her close the door behind her.

I heard a deep, heavy sigh, and I looked back at the old man. Suddenly, my heart seemed to have stopped beating. I leaned over and picked up his hand. I could feel no pulse at all. I leaned a little closer to gaze once more into his staring eyes. And then, gently, I brushed my fingers over them, closing his eyelids.

I stood looking down at him. Then, from where I don't know, a chill laced up my back. Without thought, I extended my left hand, and the sleeve of my coat slid back across my watch.

To the second.

☠

I drove back to Mary's house, unable to get the old man's story out of my mind—or the weary acceptance in his eyes. I kept telling myself it was only a coincidence that he should have died at the stroke of midnight. Somehow, I couldn't quite convince myself.

My sister Mary opened the door. The living room was empty.

"Don't tell me the party has broken up already," I said.

☠

"Why it's not quite one o'clock."

Mary was smiling happily. "No, not broken up," she said. "It just sort of changed location."

I also smiled. "To where?"

"The hospital."

I stared at her, my mind swept blank. Then it hit me. "You mean ... Ruth?"

Mary laughed and hugged me. "You'll never guess," she giggled, "what time Ruth had the sweetest little boy ... to the second!"